A
Betrayal
Exposed

by Jane McGarry

A Betrayal Exposed
by Jane McGarry
Published by JM Books

A BETRAYAL EXPOSED
Copyright © 2022 JANE MCGARRY
ISBN 978-1-7365884-7-5
Cover Art Designed by FirdaGraphics

For the real Jane, who is missed.

Oppressive. It is the only word to describe the air on this late May day. Humidity hangs like a smothering blanket over the palace while an unforgiving sun beats down on the drooping shoulders of its inhabitants. The extreme conditions have lasted so long, King William grumpily ordered his astronomers to determine the cause of the unusual heat. In the end though, he had to concede even a monarch cannot control the weather.

"At least it will not be this hot when I get married," my sister mumbles, lazily fanning her face.

She lies with my friend, Kat, and me underneath a large oak, its shade doing little to counteract the oven-like atmosphere. I shift over to my other side. Droplets of sweat run down my back, meandering rivers against the fabric of my dress. Queen Helen has allowed us the option to forgo wearing our corsets, though some still choose to keep them on for reasons I will never fathom.

"Yes. By October, there will hopefully be an end to this infernal baking," I say, laying my open book down on my chest.

Once the royal family announced the wedding date for Harold, the crown Prince, and his betrothed, Emily Crawford, my sister and her fiancé could finally select a date of their own. Anne and Montgomery opted for a date in the fall, but this is on the back burner at the moment, since the royal wedding is only a few weeks away.

June fifteenth. A date etched in everyone's mind. Not to mention Emily reminds everyone at least a thousand times a day as if we may have forgotten; unlikely, with the constant bombardment of fabric swatches, flower arrangement ideas, and food samples. Over four hundred people will be in attendance, including some royalty from the Mainland. It will be an event not seen on my tiny island kingdom of Stewartsland in my lifetime.

Hopefully, the kingdom will get the "royal wedding fever" out of their systems, so when Liam and I eventually marry, they do not subject us to this monumental scale of planning. For just over two months now, we have known the king will announce our engagement after Harold and Emily wed. At the moment, we are thoroughly enjoying our courtship. It has been the happiest two months of my life. Some mornings I even admit to pinching myself. Being a princess seems so surreal.

Life has quieted considerably since the king named me a lady-in-waiting six months ago. From a prophecy, to a witch, to an attempt on the King's life, there was hardly a dull moment. Then there was the matter of Jocelyn Crawford, Emily's sister, who tried to get Liam for herself. For a while, it looked as though her plan may succeed. But in the end, my love and I prevailed.

"We should see about riding out to the river for a swim tomorrow to cool off," Kat suggests. "Perhaps Puck could join us."

My newest friend has found love with my oldest friend. It is heartwarming to watch them together.

"I have to check on some families in the servant's village," I remind her, "so maybe after that."

A fat bumblebee hums past my face to hover around a cluster of flowers which hang wilting from their stems. It gives up after a few moments and slowly takes off into the heavy air. Even the birds, who usually chirp away, are quiet amongst the sagging boughs of the trees. The ground is hard and dusty underfoot, desperate for much needed rain.

"How is Niobe doing these days?" Anne asks of my mentor.

My work with this woman, a healer for many castle servants, was the most surprising thing which happened to me when I was thrust into palace life. When it became clear I would not fit into the traditional roles of ladies-in-waiting, Queen Helen appointed me Niobe's assistant. And I found my calling. If I cannot have the life of a knight, then this is a most rewarding option.

"She is doing well, though she still tires easily. But I suppose that is to be expected." I idly tap the open book, which lies on my chest. I brought it here with good intentions, but it is simply too hot to concentrate on its words.

The healer was gravely wounded with a dagger last Easter, protecting the King from an assassination attempt. Lord Otto, the King's illegitimate brother, was the perpetrator. He was killed by the King's nephew, Prince Stephan, during the struggle. While the incident appears to have been the actions of a disgruntled maniac, certain facts still nag at my mind. Otto had helped from inside the castle and the identity of those people remain a mystery.

"Where is Liam this afternoon?" Anne asks, breaking my train of thought.

"With Prince Harold. A batch of wild horses arrived from the Mainland. They are assessing which ones will make good battle steeds."

"Puck was so excited this morning when I saw him," Kat pipes in.

"Yes, Liam said they rely on Puck's opinion when deciding." I say. My old friend works with the Master-of-Horse and has always had a gift with these animals. Kat beams with pride at my statement.

I pick up my book again and attempt to clear the haze in my brain. Normally, I enjoy the books my father has me read, but today the heat takes its toll.

"How can you even concentrate on that?" Anne says. "It's too hot for an interesting story, let alone a boring bunch of history."

"Actually, it's about the Battle of Winchester. Granted, it's a little-known battle, but they had an interesting strategy for being outnumbered. You see, they…"

Kat holds up her hand. "Please spare us the details. It's miserable enough out here. Anne and I do not want a lesson in battle tactics on top of it."

"Your loss," I tease. "I'll just discuss it with Father later. He will be interested."

The afternoon passes sluggishly, the sun not ready to give up its sway. We giggle and gossip while snacking on ripe strawberries, each one a succulent treat. A blue sky unfolds above us, not a cloud in sight. Only the trickling of water in a nearby fountain tinkles, its sound dulled by the humid air.

At length, it is time to prepare ourselves for dinner. We pack up the fruit and our books in a basket, then head out of the sheltered garden. Our steps are slow, but we walk arm in arm, three ladies content with the world.

Our first indication something is wrong occurs when we cross the main courtyard. A guard runs up behind us and passes as if the devil were on his heels. We watch him disappear into the palace, but soon are laughing at some little joke, the moment forgotten. Just when we are about to enter the castle, however, four guards barrel out the door, nearly knocking us off our feet. They take off in the direction the first guard came from. All four of us spin to look. As the soldiers race off, a servant rushes up to two courtiers and they converse hurriedly before the men rush off in the wake of the guards. The servant runs down the length of the courtyard and dashes into another castle door.

Something is definitely going on.

The three of us exchange a quizzical glance, then turn to walk in the direction of the commotion. We cross through two courtyards and a rose garden, so full of blooms, the smell is almost cloying. More and more people join us, some whizzing past at breakneck speed.

After clearing a high hedgerow, the stables and the wide-open fields behind them come into view. A large crowd gathers by a closed pen near the paddock. One lone horse wanders around the enclosure away from the horde, its saddle empty.

"Make way!" a voice behind us yells. Yet another guard speeds past us, the royal physician on his heels. Two physician's assistants follow, each of whom carries a large bag of supplies.

Someone is hurt.

I start to run. Liam was out here with these wild horses. In my mind, I conjure a thousand pictures of him being thrown, or trampled, or any other number of injuries he may have sustained. Sheer panic fuels me, my heart in my throat, and Anne and Kat cannot keep pace. Reaching the outskirts of the crowd, which rings the fence, I elbow my way through a sea of torsos. The mass of bodies finally breaks enough for me to see inside the pen.

My heart leaps with joy when my eyes rest on a head of beautiful ebony locks, standing unharmed in a small cluster of people just inside the fence. Liam is all right. It is the only thought I can process for a moment. Slowly, my heartbeats settle from the scare of losing him.

Everyone's stare focuses on the ground. Without thought, I climb through the stiles of the fence, barely noticing when my skirt catches. A hunk of fabric rips off, the sky-blue material sticking on a splinter of wood. When I reach Liam's side, he does not react. His eyes fixed on one spot with a disbelieving expression. My gaze follows his and I nearly cry out at the sight.

Prince Harold lies on the ground, an ugly purple bruise on his temple. The royal physician is on his knees at the Prince's side. He and his assistants work feverishly with smelling salts while shaking and calling the victim's name. His efforts are to no avail.

The crowd stands deathly silent, no one daring even the sound of a breath. Heavy air weighs down on all of us, heightening the horror with its stifling grip. Instinctively, I link hands with Liam. Puck moves next to me and puts a hand on my back.

After many minutes, the physician stills his hands. He bows his head as though this can spare him of the news he must deliver, if even for a moment. On unsteady feet, he rises and places a hand on Liam's shoulder.

"I am truly sorry, Your Highness. Prince Harold is dead."

The weather breaks in earnest the day we lay Prince Harold to rest, as if the earth itself sheds innumerable tears. After a mass in the chapel, the court somberly escorts the casket to the royal tombs. Wind-whipped rain pellets the procession. King William supports the queen on his arm, an opaque veil concealing her face. Our monarch's expression is stoic, but his red-rimmed eyes suggest private mourning.

Behind them, Liam ushers Lady Emily, who leans heavily on his arm. She became positively hysterical when she learned of her fiancé's passing two days ago. I had been called in to administer a tincture. The king's nephew, Prince Stephan, trails in their wake, leading his mother, Princess Beatrice. This must be a hard day for them given that they buried the king's brother, Prince Arthur, not even a year ago in the southern city of Prescott.

I am relegated to the crowd just behind the royal family. Though I long to be at Liam's side to console him, it is not yet my place. Instead, I huddle with Kat and Puck next to my parents. Anne walks with Montgomery's family nearby. Members of our court, along with royalty, dignitaries, and ambassadors from neighboring kingdoms follow. This is a gathering the likes of which Stewartsland has not seen and was expecting to see under much different circumstances a few weeks hence.

A sea of black, all of our faces are tear-stained from the service. Monsignor Lennon, who had baptized Prince

Harold in infancy, moved the audience with a touching tribute, his poignant words outshining his frail body. Thankfully, Brother Alastair, the self-righteous monk, is gone. After spending a good part of the past year here, he returned to Prescott after the attempt on King William's life by Lord Otto, who disguised himself as a penitent brought to the kingdom with the friar. Though Brother Alastair was not involved in the plot to harm the king, the royal family said he served as a constant reminder of troubling times. Personally, I think they just disliked him as much as I did.

The tomb lies in the center of the graveyard, a massive structure adorned with trumpeting angels. We file up a few steps and enter a square room. Prince Harold's casket rests on a large pedestal in the center. His body will be brought to the crypt below after we all leave. There he will lie with his ancestors for all eternity.

People fan out as much as possible in the confined space, shoulder to shoulder, until they press against the edges of the room. The royal family stands in front of the coffin. Monsignor Lennon leads us all in prayer. When he finishes, to my surprise, he adds, "Prince Liam would like to say a few words before we conclude."

Consoling Liam has been especially difficult for me. He feels responsible for his brother's death. Although his parents and I have repeatedly told him he bears no blame, his blue eyes are clouded with anguish. Hopefully, time will bring him some perspective and some peace. I did not know he intended to speak.

He steps forward, his white color the only bright spot against his dark coat and vest. With hands clasped in front of him, he begins, "My family and I would like to thank everyone in attendance for the compassion and support shown to us these past few days. We are overwhelmed by it."

His words echo off the cold stone which envelopes the chamber, walls which have stood through many such mournful words over the years. The prince shifts, staring at the floor and an uncomfortable pause hovers in the air. Liam draws a deep breath.

"Harold was more than just our crown prince. An exemplary son and a steadfast defender of Stewartsland, he learned at a young age to put the needs of others, of this kingdom, before his own. But to me, he was also a brother — my first playmate, my most trusted confidante, my protector. He alone walked with me on the unique path of our childhood. He alone understood the intricacies and obligations of princehood. There was a bond between us, one which can never be broken, not even by his death.

"He never once complained about the burden of leadership thrust on him by birth. He bore it with a dignity and grace well beyond his years. And now it is up to us, those left without him, to face our burden in the same way…hoping to find our way through this terrible loss in a manner worthy of his memory."

Liam's crystal blue eyes fill with unshed tears. They glisten in the wavering candle light as he bows and returns to his mother's side. She links her arm in his, while wiping tears with her free hand.

While the monsignor confers a final blessing, all heads bow down, all but mine. I cannot take my eyes off of Liam, riveted on him in my pain. He must sense my gaze and raises his face to mine. The pure anguish in his expression guts me. If only one of Niobe's potions could ease his pain, but sadly, such grief is beyond the power to remedy.

The funeral repast held after the entombing is solemn, the court still in shock by the tragic death of their crown prince. Puck, Kat, and I cluster together at one end of a long trestle table, food untouched on all of our plates. Liam and his parents left the dining hall a few moments ago. Now, many courtiers take their own leave, men with arms draped around their partners' shoulder in comfort, women dabbing their eyes with already damp handkerchiefs. At loose ends, my friends and I remain, not sure where to go or what to do.

Francis, one of my old training companions, who is now a knight, slumps down next to us. "I just can't believe Prince Harold is dead. I mean, we just had a planning meeting with him on Wednesday morning and then in the afternoon he is gone."

"I don't think anyone can quite grasp it yet," Kat says, her usual bright countenance dimmed with sadness.

"Were you there, Puck? What exactly happened?" Francis asks.

My old friend heaves a sigh. "Prince Liam was on one of the wild stallions trying to break him. Quite frankly, we were all worried about his safety, as he had already taken a hard fall. The horse was rearing violently, bucking against the reins. Near the fence, the animal kicked up a large stone just as Prince Harold bent down to grab a rope off the ground. It hit him flush in the temple. He collapsed immediately and never woke."

He has repeated this story countless times to an untold number of inquirers over the past few days. Each re-telling does not lessen the pain for any of us. It does not enable us to change the tale's ending, to stop the loss, or to evade the heartache which now permeates the kingdom. Silence fills the air while we each wallow in our own grief.

A page taps my shoulder. "Excuse me, Miss Davenport, Prince Liam requests your presence. I have come to escort you."

Rising, I bid my companions farewell and follow the young man out of the dining hall and through a labyrinth of corridors. After a few turns, I am pretty sure where we head, so I am not surprised when he stops outside the door to an old planning room in a remote section of the castle. It is a frequent haunt of mine and my friends. We have dubbed it the War Room.

The page bows, then scurries off for his next assignment while I push open the door. Adam, Liam's guard, sits beneath a window, an unopened book resting on his lap. He looks down the long room, a distraught expression on his face, to where Liam stands in a doorway open to a courtyard.

Slowly, I walk toward my prince. He has removed the jacket and vest he wore to the funeral and stands in a white tunic with the neck untied and the sleeves pushed up. Wrapping one arm around him, I lean against his side. Adam quietly leaves the room. Rain falls steadily, forming pools in the lower sections of the courtyard. The drops patter in an unfaltering rhythm. A stiff breeze spritzes our faces, but Liam barely reacts. His eyes stare unseeing into the distance.

I feel ill-equipped to help him. Up until now, the worst tragedy in my life was the death of my beloved grandmother when I was eleven. Though it hurt tremendously, I had the comfort of knowing she had lived a long, full life. The same cannot be said for Prince Harold.

The magnitude of his passing eclipses anything I have ever experienced.

"Liam, I am so sorry. I feel so helpless. What can I do?"

"There is nothing you can do. There is nothing anyone can do. As I said, we all just have to go on as best we can and pray time will heal the pain." His words sound hollow, as though he does not even believe them himself. My heart shatters at the hopelessness in them.

"I am here for you, whatever you need," I whisper.

"That is my only comfort," he replies, pulling me into an embrace.

We stay this way for a long time, the endless rain pouring down outside. There are no words to ease the burden on his heart. All I can do is stand by him through this storm and hope eventually the clouds part. Liam and I weathered a lot earlier this year—my adjustment to palace life, the prophecy about danger to his father, and the eventual attempt on King William's life by a resentful step brother.

Yet, these last two months have been joyful. Once the king allowed Liam to publicly court me, our relationship flourished. What started as the hopeful bud of new love has blossomed into a partnership based on affection, loyalty and trust, a true appreciation of who the other is at the core. My worries the kingdom would look unfavorable on the match were unfounded; the reaction has been largely positive.

Harold's death is the first true obstacle we have encountered. I have the utmost faith in our ability to get through it. We are always stronger together than apart. However, one thought eats away at my surety—Liam is now heir to the throne, which makes me heir to the queen. It is a daunting prospect, one which keeps gnawing at the recesses of my brain. There is no precedent for an untitled woman to ascend to the throne. The thought scares me.

As if sensing my unease, Liam's grip tightens. "As long as I have you by my side, Olivia, there isn't anything I can't face."

I pray he is right.

"If you are too tired, child, this can wait until tomorrow," Niobe says, her bony hand stroking my hair.

The sun shines brightly outside this morning. Were it not for the mud and the lingering puddles, one would never imagine the torrents which fell yesterday. I shift in my seat at the workbench, a variety of bottles and containers needed for the tincture I prepare at arm's reach.

"Tell that to Becky," I joke, grabbing a vial from the top shelf, "she likely does not want to spend another day with morning sickness."

It is these small remedies we can provide the servants in the village which make my work with Niobe so enjoyable. Her knowledge and skill help countless people each day. I am thankful for the day Queen Helen asked me to be her assistant. It was when I finally found a meaningful place at the palace.

"Yesterday must have been difficult. Remember, take care of yourself first, if you want the strength to take care of others."

"Actually, I think I would go mad if I weren't here. Work gives me something to focus on so I can keep my mind off of everything else," I confide, my hands twirling the brewer's yeast around the vial of water while it slowly dissolves.

"Yes," she murmurs. "I find the same is true."

Niobe has surprised everyone with the swiftness of her recuperation from a grave chest wound. Although not back to her full strength yet, she improves each day. Her fighting spirit is inspiring.

Once the remedy is mixed, I nestle the vial in a basket filled with other tinctures, ointments, and poultices to bring to the village. Then I review my list to make sure no one's treatment is missing. Satisfied with the basket's contents, I cover it with a cloth, but not before tucking some peppermint sticks in, a hidden treat for sick or hurt children.

"It is not nearly as humid today as it has been, Niobe," I state, hanging my apron on a peg. "Do you want to come with me?"

"All right," she replies after a moment's consideration, "though I may not last for the entirety of your rounds."

"We both know anyone will welcome you gladly should you need to sit a spell." She smiles as I wrap a light shawl around her frail shoulders.

They venerate the healer in the village, having treated nearly every family. These last two months there have been countless inquiries about her recovery and countless gifts bestowed on her. Even the nobility of the court, who previously discounted her as some crazy vice of the king, are concerned with her progress.

Linking elbows with her, I guide us out the door into the bright sunlight. Fragmented strips of clouds pass across the deep blue sky like broad white paint strokes. In the village, rejuvenated flowers bloom in garden beds and window boxes, vivid pops of color against whitewashed clapboards. My friend looks startlingly pale against the vibrant hues all around us. Hopefully, the fresh air will bring some color back to her cheeks.

We stop in front of a modest cottage whose door stands open. Two small girls play on the step outside with some cornhusk dolls. Their eyes light up at the sight of Niobe and they practically tackle her. I tighten my grip so they will not knock her flying.

Becky, their mother, appears in the doorway, a needle in one hand and a basket of mending in the other. Her complexion is the color of dingy sheets and dark hollows frame her eyes.

"Here is the remedy for your morning sickness." I hold out the vial to her. "Take a half a teaspoon three times a day.

"Thank you. I don't know who decided on the term 'morning' sickness when 'all day' sickness would have been far more accurate. At least with this one." She instinctively rubs her belly, still too flat to reveal its secret. "It is nice to see you out and about, Niobe," she adds, walking down the one step to embrace the healer.

Niobe garners a lot of attention on her trip. People come out to see her and wish her well. Children tug on her skirt and she gently pats their heads. Our progress is slow, but thankfully, there are few ailments to tend to today. The last stop is at the house of Mae Simpson, whose son, Franklin, is the beau of my handmaiden, Sadie. She ushers us inside and insists we sit with her for a piece of fresh-baked pie. At the large table, I watch as my friend heartily enjoys her slice.

When we head back to her chambers, her mismatched eyes, one blue, one green, glow in a way I have not seen since her injury. I am grateful she joined me today. Once inside, I empty the basket, setting the used vials aside to be washed, then tidy up the workbench, clearing off the debris and shelving some small jars. Finally, I write a list of remedies we will need for tomorrow.

"Would you like to work on some entries for the book?" I ask. It had taken some coaxing, but I finally convinced her to record her vast knowledge for future reference. This task has helped her pass many days when she was still bedridden.

"Not today, child. I am worn out from our excursion and need to go lie down. Why don't you go spend time with that handsome prince of yours?"

"All right," I agree, but see her settled into bed before leaving.

I am unsure where Liam is this afternoon, so I stroll down to the stables. Puck is there combing down one of the stallions, his methodical strokes enjoyed by the animal, who gnaws on some hay. He motions me over.

"Has Liam been here today?" I question.

"He was here this morning. He was going to ride, but the king summoned him before we could get his horse saddled up. He hasn't been back." Puck stands, brushing horsehair from his pants.

"Oh." If he is with the king, he won't be able to see me anyway. I lean against the back of the stall and shut my eyes. The thought I have kept at bay all morning—the need to see Liam, to comfort him—eats at my gut like an insatiable creature, feelings of sorrow and inadequacy left in the wake of its feast. Words spill from my mouth. "He feels so guilty, Puck. I don't know how to help him."

Puck comes to my side, gently placing his hand on my arm. "I'm not sure there is anything you can do. Just give it time."

"Time!" I yell. "I am sick of everyone saying to give it time. Time takes too long, time makes me feel useless, time is too ambiguous a phrase. How long? How long does it take? Because the waiting is excruciating."

My old friend lets me rant, a stoic expression on his face. He is one person I can blurt out all my fears to, someone who will always listen but never judge. The horse whinnies and shakes his tail impatiently, not fond of my shouting. Puck leads him back to his stall, then returns and plops down on a nearby hay bale.

"You can't always fix everything right away, Livy. There are some things that just are not within people's power. You know it's true."

"Yes," I stubbornly agree, the thought not making me feel any better while I sink down next to him.

He ladles some water from a bucket and takes a long drink. When he offers it to me, I shake my head. Neither drink nor food will help the gnawing in my stomach. We sit in silence for a few minutes, the buzzing of flies blending with an occasional snort from one of the stalls. A warm cross breeze filters through the building, sending errant strands of hay aloft. It is actually a beautiful day, but the world seems dulled by my grief and worry.

"How are things with you and Kat?" I finally ask, in an attempt to change the subject and my mood.

"Great," he replies, his face lighting up with a huge grin. "Don't tell her, but I am trying to save up enough money these next few months so I can make her an offer of marriage."

"Oh Puck, that's wonderful," I fling my arms around his neck, for a moment my cares forgotten.

"Thanks, Livy. This job is the best thing that ever happened to me, besides Kat, of course. I finally found my place in the world and I owe it all to you."

We embrace again and I am reminded of a simpler time when Puck and I sparred with wooden swords, fished in the creek, and made forts in the forest. All the while, we couldn't wait to grow up. Now, I wish I could go back and tell those two children to enjoy every minute they had before adulthood showed up with its burdens. But for this brief moment, I cling to the carefree memories of childhood. The sound of hoofbeats approaching the stables brings me back to reality.

"Looks like Prince Stephan's party is back from their picnic. I'll need to help them," Puck says, rising from his seat.

"All right." I rise, ready to depart. "Wait…Prince Stephan went on a picnic the day after Prince Harold's funeral?"

Puck shrugs. "He said he wanted to take all the ladies' minds off of the tragic event."

"Huh," is the only response I can manage. It does not seem like the time for socializing. The wound is still too raw. I did not know Harold well, but I liked him. Prince Stephan was his cousin, for goodness sake. Baffled by the whole thought, I leave my friend to his work.

At dinner, I hear all about the picnic from Emily and some other members of her entourage, the Wolf Pack, as I have dubbed them. Since the prince's passing, his fiancé has outdone herself in mourning. Today is no exception. Her cohorts, Gretchen and Elaine, sit on either side of her, each with a consoling hand on her arm.

"It was so good of Prince Stephan to take us out today," she sniffs, a handkerchief ready in hand, "these last few have been…so…difficult." She dissolves into tears while her friends coo and comfort her.

People at other tables look over, eyes full of sympathy for the poor young woman who lost her love. I know I should be more compassionate, but there is something less than genuine about her grief, as though she ramps it up for attention; though my dislike for her sister, Jocelyn, certainly taints my view of Emily. I cast a side-long glance at Anne, who sits beside me. Anne's eyes are misty. Perhaps I am mistaken. Perhaps melodrama is the only way Emily knows how to express her emotions.

Kat scurries in and eases down on the other side of me. She hastily brushes some loose strands of hair behind her ears and smoothes out her skirt. Stray pieces of hay drop to the floor.

"Having some fun in the stables?" I tease.

"Ha ha. Yes, I was there, but then a rider arrived with a message for the king and Puck had to attend to his tired horse."

"What was the message about?" I ask, my senses instantly heightened.

"Oddly, the man didn't tell a random girl in the stable the information he carried to our monarch," she replies sarcastically.

I will have to find out from Liam. The whole day has passed without me seeing him. We have not been apart for more than one day since King William allowed our courtship. In fact, yesterday, he specifically said if nothing else, he would be at dinner today. A sick hollow grows in my stomach. What if something is wrong? He has been so distant since his brother's death. What if his feelings for me are affected somehow? A million fearful scenarios of me losing him fill my mind. Suddenly, I feel helpless and vulnerable sitting here without him.

Anne nudges me. "Are you listening to me? I asked you how Niobe was feeling?" The paranoia dissipates and flutters away for the moment.

But at night, when I blow out my candle and settle into bed, the uncertainty creeps back in. I try mightily to keep my uneasiness at bay while I dissect every conversation and interaction the two of us have had in the past few days. What if I said or did the wrong thing? Would it be magnified by his grief? Had Harold's loss taken the part of him able to love someone away? Obsessive thoughts of life without Liam torment me in the still darkness of the room until I fall into a restless sleep.

After a fitful night, I rise early and quietly dress myself. Anne rolls over in our shared bed and pulls the covers tighter around her. Sadie, our maid, will not be here for another hour, but I want to go to Niobe's where at least my time can be productive. After stepping into a loose day dress, I twist my hair into a hasty bun and secure it with some pins. A faint shaft of light spills into the room from the crack between the shutters.

When I open the door to leave, I almost collide with a page. We both let out startled gasps which echo off the stone walls of the hallway. The boy recomposes himself and holds out a note. I recognize Liam's seal. As the messenger hurries away, I tear open the envelope.

Olivia–
I am sorry I did not get to see you yesterday. My father wanted to meet to discuss matters of the kingdom and it went late into the evening.
Meet me in the War Room today at 2.
I missed you.
All my love,
Liam

His words lift the burden weighing down my heart. At least I know he was not avoiding me on purpose. My steps feel lighter on the way to the healer's chambers. The dawn glows pink and orange all around me. Birds chirp, flittering from tree to tree. When I reach Niobe's door, a light wind carries the aroma of the nearby herb garden, a fusion of scents from sweet to woodsy. My uneasiness from last night seems unfounded and I am surprised I let my emotions get the better of me.

I spend the morning mixing tinctures and assembling poultices. Niobe does not accompany me to the village. Yesterday's visit has left her too tired. Besides, the weather is becoming stifling again, the oppressive humidity back full force in the heat of the mid-morning sun. I hasten through my rounds, then return to the chamber just before two o'clock, where I clean up the workbench and see Niobe safely to her bed for a nap. Finally, it is time to see Liam.

Sweat beads on my brow on the way over, the pleasantness of this morning's walk obliterated by the unforgiving rays of the sun. By the time I reach my destination, my damp dress sticks to my back and my bun sways low and limp against my neck. It is a relief to step into the War Room, which remains somewhat cool, its north facing stones not absorbing the full brunt of the sun. The doors at either end stand open, creating a small cross breeze for its occupants.

Adam sits in his usual chair, but today a plump baby sits on a blanket at his feet. "I have some company today," the guard says.

"Hi, Charlie," I coo, kneeling down next to the little boy. He waves his chubby hands over his head and squeals.

"Adam, he is so cute. How old is he now?"

"He will be nine months next week," Adam beams. "He can sit by himself and crawl too. Give him a chance, you'll see."

"Where is Liza?" It is odd the boy is not with his mother.

"She had to go tend her parents, who both contracted some sort of stomach illness during the night. So, I took him to let him see what his father does all day."

"Yes," Liam chimes in from the other end of the room, "break him in so he knows the position for Olivia's and my children."

Adam and I laugh, and Liam almost smiles. Almost.

I stroll down and embrace him, my head resting familiarly on his shoulder. His powerful arms wrap around me and I feel anchored to the world once again.

"I am sorry about yesterday," he begins, "my father was quite long-winded."

"That's all right," I assure him. "He has a lot on his mind. You both do."

"Thank you for understanding," he sighs and kisses the top of my head.

We remain interlocked for a few moments, simply enjoying one another's presence. He smells of the balsam in his soap and the musk from his cologne. It calms me to be this close to him, to feel our hearts beating together, as though nothing can ever go wrong.

"Kat said a message arrived last night." Suddenly, the thought came to mind.

"Yes. There is some unrest in the north again. Raiders plague the mining communities on the coast. Another soldier was killed. Your father and Prince Stephan joined my father and me in the meeting to discuss the latest news.

Such roving bands of pillagers keep attacking the coastal villages since the fall of Lindenwood. Several times, the king has sent troops up to restore order and a handful of them remain, but not enough to patrol the entire shoreline.

The quarries and surrounding settlements provide easy victims for the raiders, who can quickly escape via sea to the Mainland."

"What will be done? Perhaps it is time to settle an entire squadron up there permanently," I suggest.

"Yes, that was your father's solution, but Prince Stephan was adamant we needed to go up there ourselves to survey the situation personally."

"I suppose that makes sense," I muse, though given the recent loss of the crown-prince, not entirely necessary. A well-appointed group of men could certainly be trusted to bring information back to the king. Father would not want to put any more worry on the monarch's shoulders right now.

"Actually, your father and Prince Stephan argued over several things yesterday. My father finally dismissed us, saying he wanted the night to think about it. That is unlike him. He is normally so decisive." I hear the worry in his tone.

"Well, he is grieving, and the wound is still new. I wouldn't expect him to be himself after losing a son." I rub Liam's shoulders.

"Yes, I suppose we have all been hit hard," Liam sighs.

I am surprised my father and Prince Stephan butted heads. It will be interesting to hear Father's account of the meeting. It is unlike him to dispute openly with a member of the royal family. Prince Harold's death must have taken its toll on Father as well.

There is a loud rap at the door and a page enters. He scans the room nervously. When his eyes fall on Liam, he states, "His Majesty, King William, requests the presence of Prince Liam and Miss Olivia Davenport immediately."

Liam and I exchange a surprised glance. Adam stands and scoops up Charlie, who screams in protest.

"Very well," Liam says, and the boy bows and waits for us to accompany him. "Adam, just stay here with your son. I am sure this will not take long."

"Thank you, Your Highness." Adam's shoulders sag in relief at not having to bring a screaming child into the king's company. He deposits Charlie back down on the rug, where the boy happily bangs some blocks together.

"Come, my love." He takes my arm and escorts me from the room, seeming unfazed by the summons.

With each step we take, dread builds in my body. What could the king want with both of us? A pang in my gut tells me it can be nothing good. My palms begin to sweat and my heart pounds against my ribs. Liam strolls along casually, greeting different courtiers as we pass. I want to share my concern with him, but somehow, I cannot force out the words, so I simply glide next to him mechanically.

The page leads us to a private reception room adjacent to the royal family's wing. When the door opens, I feel as though an abyss opens at my feet. I freeze. Liam looks at me questioningly.

"Come in, you two," the king's voice booms. My feet move again at the order.

There is a large table in the room, but neither of its occupants sits. The king paces back and forth behind its long side, while the queen stands against the wall, a distressed expression on her face.

"What can we do for you, Your Majesty?" Liam asks, taking my sweaty hand in his steady one, as though finally sensing the dread I feel.

The monarch stops mid-way down the table. He is quiet for a moment before he speaks. "There is no easy way to say this, and I hope you both understand I did not come to this decision lightly."

My stomach officially crashes to my toes.

"The untimely passing of your brother has forced me to reconsider some matters."

The moment these words pass his lips, I know what is coming. Desperately, I will him not to say anything more. Liam's grip on my hand tightens.

"Liam, you are heir to the throne now. For the good of the kingdom, I can no longer condone your marriage to Miss Davenport. Your union will need to be a more strategic pairing."

"A strategic pairing?" Liam sneers. "What am I? A pawn in your chess game?'

"No, you are the future king of Stewartsland now. Your life is about fulfilling that obligation."

Any thought of a response from me fades as my ability to speak dissolves. In fact, I can barely breathe, as though two clenched fists squeeze the air out of my lungs. In a way, I feel disembodied, as if I watch this scene happen to someone else. The silence in the room throbs with anger and disbelief.

"No," Liam states emphatically.

"No?"

"No." He releases my hand and leans on the table, squaring his shoulders.

"You do not get the luxury of saying no, young man," King William orders, standing at his full height, ready to challenge his son.

The room blurs as my eyes fill with tears and still, I am unable to utter a syllable. Somehow, I knew this was coming, knew it was inevitable, knew what Liam and I shared was too magical to last.

"Well, I *am* saying no. I will marry Olivia," Liam shouts, now nose to nose with his father.

"Enough," the king hollers, slamming his hands on the table and I jump, "you will do as I say, or I will send her away!"

"You will not take her from me. I won't let you," Liam chokes, his voice filled with the sheer desperation which floods my entire body.

"I think we all need to calm down," Queen Helen interjects, finally stepping from the wall to her husband's side.

The king sighs and turns away from his son. Liam's shoulders sag in despair. His mother looks at him, her face full of sympathy. I want to put my arms around him, to comfort him, but I stand rooted to my spot, still feeling like an observer rather than a participant in the room's event.

"Perhaps we should all sleep on this and discuss it anew in the morning," Helen suggests.

King William pinches the bridge of his nose. "In the morning, I was going to ask Liam to arrange for a party to go north to check out the unrest in the mining communities."

"Then, let us table the whole topic until he returns. We are all still plagued by grief over Harold and should hold off on any momentous decisions."

"A day's time will not change my mind," the monarch assures us. "I have to put the kingdom first, so does Liam."

"Not without Olivia," Liam asserts

Queen Helen sighs. "Please both of you, emotions are too high now. Just wait."

Her words sound rational and would seem the sensible course of action. The men nod in reluctant agreement, though somehow, I see neither one of them changing their opinion. I should be happy it buys us some time to think of counterarguments, but deep inside I know it will not matter. King William's reasoning has guided kingdoms throughout his reign. With Liam the sole heir, it will depend on his offspring to carry on the family's legacy. There is no precedent for a woman of my stature to be his wife, a fact more easily overlooked when Prince Harold was alive. Still, I feel betrayed to the core by the king's actions.

"Then if you will excuse us, we will be going." Liam's tone could freeze a lake.

He takes my hand and escorts me out of the room, then down several hallways until we are in a secluded nook near his room. Gently, he wipes the tears from my eyes.

"Don't worry, Olivia. I will take care of this." He wraps me in an embrace.

Still, I have no words. The very real prospect of losing Liam has stolen them away.

The next day dawns bright and sunny. For a brief instant, when I first wake, I do not remember the events of yesterday. In this blissful moment, my heart is light, but then the dead weight of my troubles drops back down full force on my chest. I am unusually quiet while I dress. Anne, who was filled in on the details last night, watches me, a distressed look on her face, but offers no sentiments of comfort. It is just as well; her words would feel hollow anyway.

When we exit our room to go to breakfast, another door opens in the hallway. Emily emerges with Gretchen and Elaine on either side. They each hold an arm consolingly while she sighs, "So this will be my last breakfast here. So many memories…I will miss you both so much."

"Are you leaving us, Emily?" Anne asks, our paths meeting in the corridor. In the chunk of room visible through the still opened door, a flurry of activity occurs inside. Maids bustle to and fro, garments and trinkets in hand. Numerous trunks, their lids gaping like hungry mouths, stand ready to accept these deposits.

"Why, yes," she says, pausing dramatically with teary eyes, "it is just too hard to be here. Everything reminds me of my dear Harold. I travel back to my home in the south this afternoon. Then I will try to go on with my life."

At this point, she dissolves into a fit of small choking sobs. Other Wolf Pack members, who have joined us in the hall, comfort her and lead her away. Anne shrugs slightly at me before following them. A trunk slams shut, its lock clicking into place with a resounding finality.

After a few steps, I grab my sister's arm to stop her. "I just can't deal with Emily this morning. I think I'll pass on breakfast."

"All right," Anne replies, taking my hand in concern, "try not to worry, Liv. I'm sure everything will work out."

"Thanks," I mumble to her retreating figure.

My plan is to go to Niobe's, maybe cut through the kitchen to grab a sweet roll. I turn down a side passageway to head in this direction, but when I get outside, I alter course and head for the stables instead. Sometimes you just need to talk to your best friend.

Cotton candy clouds dot a pristine blue sky, which float slowly past, as if they too want to enjoy the beautiful sunshine. My head is a muddle of thoughts, jumping from one to another, but each too slippery to fully grasp. The only constant is the deep ache in my heart. Smells of hay and manure intensify the closer my steps come to the stables.

A flurry of activity transpires in and around the building. Grooms brush horses, their tails flicking in content. Stable boys run back and forth with saddle bags or check for tack, which need repairing. Puck leads a gelding out into the paddock. When he spots me, he leads the animal to the fence to meet me.

"Busy morning?" I ask, giving the horse's nose a rub.

"Yes actually. We are getting the horses ready for the Princes' trip north. They hope to leave before noon. What brings you by?"

"Oh, nothing," I answer, not wanting to bother my friend when he has more pressing matters to attend to. How could I have forgotten about Liam's mission?

My old friend raises an eyebrow. "Livy, how long have we known each other? I can tell by your eyes something is wrong."

"I suppose that is the downfall of having a lifelong friend—nothing gets past them."

Briefly, I fill him in on what occurred with the king. He is silent for a few moments, his face pinched in concentration. I know he will give me an honest opinion; there will be no sugar-coating from Puck. It is the reason I came here. The horse nudges my hands for more attention while I wait.

"I understand how much this worries you," he starts, "but I think King William acts out of grief. The longer you can forestall any decision, the more likely he is to change his mind."

"I hope so. He sounded pretty set in his choice."

"At least now Prince Liam will be gone for a few days. That buys you time and will allow tensions to settle down between him and his father. And it gives you and I time to brainstorm a compelling argument in your favor."

He winks and I have to smile. The Master-of Horse calls out for him. "Now let me get back to work. And don't worry," he calls over his shoulder. The gelding watches him before it retreats into the paddock to graze. Puck is the third person to tell me not to worry, yet it does nothing to alleviate my growing disquiet. With a heavy sigh, I make my way to the healer's chambers.

I spend the rest of my morning at Niobe's preparing some tinctures and poultices. She declines my offer to join me on my rounds, but allows me to settle her on a chair under a tree for some fresh air. Returning from the village, she dozes in it, a peaceful look on her face. Earlier, I am sure she sensed my anxiety, but thankfully did not press me. If I have to explain my dilemma to one more person, I fear I will fall apart.

Around noon, I decide to leave Niobe in her napping spot and head back to the stables, hoping to see Liam before he departs. I come over the small rise and spot a large party of men milling about the buildings. Horses stand at intervals, tails swooshing briskly in the warm air, while stable hands saddle them up. My eyes settle on Liam, who stands confidently by his steed. His posture shows none of the worry which currently eats away at my soul an agonizing inch at a time. When he sees me, his face lights up. It is impossible not to smile back, despite all my unease.

"I was hoping you would come," he whispers in my ear after a quick kiss. Instantly, I look around to see if anyone noticed, unsure the king would approve of this show of affection.

Liam takes my face in his hands. "Don't."

"Don't what?"

"Don't act like we are doing something wrong. Don't spend my time away fretting. And most importantly, don't think this will not all work out. It will. All right?"

He seems so sure. He always does about life working out just the way you want it to. I try to muster the strength to match his optimism.

"Alright," I reassure him, leaning into his arms. Here it feels as though he is right, as though nothing could ever keep us apart.

"We really should be going," a voice says behind us. Prince Stephan stands a few feet away. "Always lovely to see you, Olivia." He holds out a hand and I have no choice but to place mine in his. He raises it to his lips. It is hard to hide the feeling of disgust which courses through me. There is something about this man rubs me the wrong way.

"We don't want those mercenaries getting too far ahead of us, do we, Prince Liam?" Though his tone is joking, I sense an underlying impatience. A perfunctory smile fills his face. He truly does not have the personality of his cousins...well, cousin now.

"I am going to wish my father farewell." I excuse myself.

Father stands at the front of the makeshift caravan, speaking with a soldier I do not recognize. Of the twenty or so men assembled, I only know a handful. The others hail from Prescott and traveled here with Prince Stephan. Albert, one of my classmates, double checks his saddlebags. He looks up and waves, excitement apparent in his eyes. For a second, a wave of envy floats over me. I miss my days of training, of believing it could actually be my life.

The soldier walks away when I approach, and a broad grin fills my father's face. "Hello, Livy." He pulls me into a bear hug. "I was hoping to see you before we left."

"How long do you think you will be gone?"

"Hard to say until I know what we are dealing with. At best a week," he surmises, his brow furrowing into creases all too familiar to me.

"Why are so many of Prince Stephan's men on this mission?"

"He asked that they make this trip since they have been sitting fairly idle since their arrival. I thought it a prudent idea to leave more of my own men with King William, given his current state of grief. If any difficulties arise here, Sir Michael will be of more use at the king's side than mine."

"That makes sense, I guess," I reply, yet I have an odd, uneasy feeling about it.

Father must perceive my misgivings. "I assure you, sweetheart, Prince Arthur trained the men in Prescott well." That was true enough. Prince Stephan' s late father had the reputation of a savvy battle strategist.

"You're right. I'll just miss you." I place my hand affectionately on his arm.

"And your prince, no doubt," he teases, and I smile. "All right then, try to stay out of trouble. I'll see you on our return. I love you."

"I love you too, Father," I whisper, and he kisses the top of my head.

Prince Stephan saddles up and orders the men into formation while I head back over to Liam. Adam has joined him. It comforts me to know his friend will be at his side. We exchange quick regards. "Don't worry, Adam, I will keep an eye on Liza and Charlie while you are gone."

"Thanks, Miss Olivia." He swings his leg over the horse's back and trots off to the other men, leaving Liam and me as alone as possible.

"Don't worry," my prince says, drawing me into his arms again, "I'll be back before you know it with lots of good stories to share. Maybe I will even run into Athos."

The mention of the outlaw who helped us so much on our mission last fall brings a smile to my face. He has remained a true and loyal friend to us both.

"I will be quite jealous if you do." I joke, but then turn serious. "Just promise to come back to me in one piece."

"I promise and then we will work everything out with my father."

We share as passionate of a kiss as we dare with so many spectators before he mounts his steed. "Oh, and try to stay out of trouble."

"Well, I can't make any promises," I kid. He knows me as well as my father does.

"I love you, Olivia."

"I love you too." With one last touch of my hair, he swings around to join the group. They move off in an orderly fashion down a path from the stables to the main road, where they round a corner and disappear. For a long time, I watch the empty space, a strange feeling of dread in my stomach. Despite Liam's certainty, I fear nothing will ever be the same.

6

When I arrive at Queen Helen's reception room, there is a flurry of activity, the buzz of a crowd audible even before I round the last corner. At her door, ladies and servants spill out into the hallway. They move deferentially to make room for me, my status among them increased since Liam courts me publicly. I navigate my way through the sea of bodies to see what the commotion is about.

Emily stands in the middle of the room, flanked by Gretchen and Elaine. Every head turns in her direction to listen to her speak. "I will never be able to thank all of you enough for all you have done for me. I always felt so welcome here. It would have been my honor to have been your princess," she beams, clearly enjoying the spotlight. "As I am sure, it would have been yours. While I am leaving today, I am sure I will see all of you together again soon. Adelina is like a second home to me now."

Kat catches my eye from across the room and we share a knowing look, which would have been an eye roll had we been alone. Emily dabs at her eyes with her handkerchief, although there are no discernible tears and, more striking to me, no words about her recently deceased fiancé.

The small audience applauds, then circle around her to offer individual goodbyes, which she laps up like a kitten with a saucer of milk. I use the opportunity to skirt the edge of the room, stopping by Kat's side. There has been no opportunity to tell her about yesterday's demand from the king. Hopefully, she can help me gain some perspective.

"I heard a group traveled north to Lindenwood, well, what used to be Lindenwood. Was Liam among them?" she asks, before I can say anything.

"Yes. They just left not thirty minutes ago." I must look bereft because she squeezes my arm.

"Don't worry. He will be back before you know it."

The room slowly clears, servants returning to their duties, ladies dispersing into small groups. Emily walks over to us in all her haughtiness, her minions trailing in her wake. "Well, I suppose this is goodbye," she drawls out.

"Farewell, Emily. I am sorry you must leave us under these tragic circumstances. At least you will have the comfort or your family in Prescott," Kat consoles.

"Yes, my family…" she half mumbles.

"We are all truly sorry for your loss. Best wishes to you, Emily," I offer.

She draws herself up in the self-important manner I despise. "And best wishes to you as well, Olivia. I have a feeling you are going to need them." She gives me a mock bow of her head, then leaves the room.

"What on earth is that supposed to mean?" Kat queries, her brow pinched in annoyance.

Somehow, Emily must know of the conversation Liam and I had with King William. It shouldn't surprise me. That woman chases gossip like a dog chases its tail. Surely some word of what took place had filtered down among the staff, eventually snaking its way to her ear.

"I think I know," I comment to my friend. "I have something to tell you."

We settle into the window seat, the very place I met Kat all those months ago when I felt lost and alone in my new home. Now, the room has emptied, even the queen tending to other duties. Detail by detail, I fill her in on all King William, Queen Helen and Liam said just today.

"Puck thinks the king's decision is clouded by grief and that he will come around," I conclude.

"Oh, he simply must," Kat cries, "You and Liam were made for each other." She gently takes my hands, tries to console the palpable worry I feel. "After all, think of what you two have been through already and you have kept your relationship intact. This is just another bump in the road. I'm sure of it."

"Hopefully, you are right," I counter, wishing I could bottle some of my friend's optimism.

"Come on," she stands and tugs me up with her, "it's a pleasant day. Let's have a walk around the gardens and maybe we can visit Puck at the stables. A good spar will cheer you up."

We head down the hall and out into the beautiful late morning sun, but it does little to cast the dark clouds from my mind.

⁘

The next few days pass without incident. My work in the village keeps my mornings busy. Niobe listens sympathetically to my story and my worries and though she tells me not to fret, she seems unusually distracted. I write it off to a combination of her injury and the heat.

Puck, Kat, and I laze away the afternoons in the shade of the stables or down by the banks of a nearby stream. The court seems unable to regroup after the Prince's death and the subsequent abandonment of the wedding plans. So much recent time and effort had gone into so many of its different aspects, from food ordering, to dressmaking, to guest housing preparation. There is a definite mourning of this loss as well.

On the fourth day after Liam's departure, I rise somewhat groggy. Massive thunderstorms had rocked the sky overnight, disturbing both mine and Anne's sleep. However, when I step outside, the air is positively refreshing, with a pleasant breeze lifting my hair. A dewy coat covers all surfaces, glinting off the hard stone walls and sparkling on every blade of grass in the early morning sun. The stifling weather had been so prevalent, one almost forgot how uplifting a respite could be.

Mary, a kitchen maid, greets me when I cut through her domain on my way to Niobe's.

"Good day, Miss Olivia. Have a sweet roll." She extends a basket, steam still wafting from them.

"Thanks. It is such a beautiful morning."

"Yes," she agrees, shaping a risen mound of dough into a loaf pan. "After that racket last night, it is like a day sent by angels."

What a perfect description, I think, a bit of extra spring in my step. Niobe sits at her workbench when I arrive, but rather than her usual busy hands, she stares blankly ahead, not even turning when I enter.

"Are you all right?" I question, while retrieving my apron off its peg and securing it around my waist.

After a long pause, she mumbles, "Honestly, I don't know."

"Are you ill?" I ask, rushing to her side where I feel her forehead and check her pulse. Both are normal.

"No," she replies, brushing away my hands, "I feel uneasy, as though some misfortune hangs over this court, but I cannot gain any clarity about it. Yet, I sense it somehow concerns you."

An icy feeling of dread fills me from the toes up. Niobe has had numerous predictions over the years which have been astonishingly accurate. Could her unease be an indicator all will not go smoothly for Liam and me? Will I find myself banished to the south? My heart flutters like a caged bird against my ribcage.

"Let me make you some tea and then we can prepare the day's remedies." I offer in a tone far calmer than my insides feel.

The drink soothes the healer and she is like her old self when she explains how to mix a tincture for gout. While she shows me how to grind ginger to a specific consistency, the door bangs open. We both look up with a start to see the culprit—a tiny girl with a frantic look on her face. All she manages to say is, "Help…Mama needs help."

Niobe is out of her seat in a split second. She grabs a small wicker basket set in the middle of one shelf. I remember what it is for about the same time my mind registers the child is Becky's daughter. We make it to their house quicker than I would ever imagine my old friend could move. The child runs behind us, small sobs escaping her frightened body. Once inside, we find Becky lying on the floor, her other daughter clinging to her hand.

"I don't know what happened," she pants through obvious pain. "I was fine when all of a sudden a terrible cramp seized me."

Gently, I lead the little girl outside, where her sister joins her forlornly on the front steps.

"Niobe needs some quiet time to help your mama. Can you both sit out here and be good for a little bit?"

Four wide eyes nod back at me. Fear etches their faces, but I don't know what comfort to offer them. A young woman from the house next door approaches. She saw us arrive and now pieces together what transpires.

"I'll keep an eye on them. Come girls; want to help me make a pie?"

The girls rise tentatively but follow her. I nod in thanks at her and return inside.

Niobe has moved the patient to the bed in the other room and props some pillows behind her. There is a deep red stain on the living room floor where she had been. While the healer performs her examination, I pull a chair next to the bed and take Becky's hand, though I am not sure if the shaking is from her or me.

Finally, Niobe pulls the blankets down and says, "It looks like a clean loss. I will give you a tincture to drink, which should clean you out the rest of the way. You should recover quickly after that."

"Will I be able to bear more children?" Becky asks, her whisper barely audible.

"I don't see why not. But for now, what you need is rest." The healer pauses a moment, then asks, "Would you like to bury it? Or would you prefer I dispose of it?"

It is then I notice a ball of cloth at the foot of the bed. Tears well in my eyes, but I know I have to hold it together for everyone's sake.

"Leave it. John and I will take care of it."

Silence hangs in the room like a suffocating fog. Niobe administers two tinctures to the patient, noting the second one is to help her sleep. Then she packs up her gear and straightens up the room. All the while, I am unable to let go of Becky's hand.

"Come, Olivia," my friend beckons. "She needs to rest now."

Slowly, almost reluctantly, I release my grip and rise. When we reach the door, Becky voices the question which most torments her mind, "Was it a boy?" Her soft voice could shatter the stoutest heart.

Niobe turns to face her. "Too soon to tell. Now rest, dear. I will check on you later today."

I don't even remember the walk back to the healer's chambers; one moment I was in Becky's house, the next, I stand at the workbench again, the invigorated feelings created by the nice weather a distant memory. Now I am the one who stares blankly ahead.

"Miscarriages are hard," Niobe acknowledges, putting her arm around my waist. "The first one you witness, especially so. But they are a part of nature. Babies unlikely to survive are expelled by the body early sometimes."

So many thoughts and feelings careen around my brain, it leaves me numb. Of course, we all know these things happen every day as a matter of course, but the unfairness of it is almost more than I can bear.

When my lip quivers with emotion, Niobe says, "There is something you want to ask. What is it?"

"*Was* it a boy?"

"Yes," she whispers sadly.

My resolve breaks and sobs wrack my body. I cry for Becky, for the lost baby, for the fragileness and unpredictability of life. Niobe holds me in her arms for a long time, before all my tears are spent.

Humidity descends again with the afternoon air, the refreshing morning but a memory. The short walk from Niobe's to the stables is enough to leave my dress clinging to my sweaty body. My spirit is so heavy, I barely notice the discomfort of the itchy fabric.

Puck is virtually alone between the Princes' departures and the weather. Two stable boys muck out the stalls while the horses are in the paddock where they huddle in the shade of some gigantic oaks. My friend inspects a bridle, head bent in careful examination of all connection points in the worn leather. He barely looks up when I arrive.

"You'll be happy to know, I've spent most of the morning concocting reasons why King William should…" he stops abruptly when he takes a closer look at me. "Livy, what happened? Were you crying over Liam?"

My eyes still feel puffy; my nose still runny. Between that and the perspiration inducing walk here, I can only imagine how frightful I look.

"One of the villagers, she…well, something sad befell her." I cannot bring myself to tell the story out loud.

"I'm sorry," he consoles, rising to pat my back. "That must be the hard part of working with Niobe."

"Yes, it is," I agree. "She knew, Puck. She knew something bad was going to happen when I arrived this morning."

The healer and I had not discussed the fact that the miscarriage was the misfortune she sensed. It involved me, after all, so surely this is what it had to be. At least, this is what I tell myself to ward off thoughts her premonition could concern Liam and me.

"Well, she is known to do that," Puck muses. "Do you feel like sparring? I certainly have the time."

"In a few minutes. Let me sit for a moment." I plop down ungraciously on a hay bale against the wall.

Puck scrutinizes one last length of the bridle, then hangs it up. He reaches for his water flask. "Here, have some." I savor a greedy gulp.

"Hello, you two." Kat's familiar voice makes us both smile.

"Hello to you," Puck responds, crossing to her side for a quick peck on the cheek. "Were you dismissed for the afternoon?"

"Yes, mercifully. Queen Helen said it was too hot to concentrate on anything."

While I get to work with Niobe, poor Kat must endure the queen's reception room. There she transcribes prayer cards and fends for herself among the Wolf Pack.

"That was kind of her," I say.

"She seemed rather distracted today. Though I suppose it's normal having just lost her son and all."

Hearing Her Highness is troubled further fuels my anxiety about Liam. She has been a staunch ally throughout my relationship with her son. What if even she cannot figure out a way to sway the king's decision on the situation?

Kat settles next to me and her eyes fill with concern. "Looks like you had a rough morning."

My resolve cracks. Becky's story tumbles out and before I can help it, I am a blubbering idiot. All the worries of the conversation with the king, Niobe's premonition, plus all my fears of losing Liam forever spill out like seeds of grain from a split sack. Kat rubs my back while Puck fetches more water. They wait for me to settle down. Neither plies me with false hope. When I finally compose myself, I wipe my eyes and nose on the sleeve of my dress. No need for manners among friends.

"I think I am ready to spar now," I volunteer.

Puck produces two wooden swords from the back of a stall, and we begin. We parry and lunge across the floor, dirt floating in small dust clouds around our feet. The exertion helps to calm my mind, the familiar physical movements somehow a balm for my nerves. After about an hour, we both collapse next to Kat, who has patiently cheered us on. Sweat beads down my back and chest. I take a swig of water, which is now lukewarm and not particularly revitalizing.

"Thanks, Puck. I feel better now."

"I'm glad," he replies.

We all sit quietly, each to our own thoughts. The heavy air envelopes us in a torpid grip, defeating any will to move on to another activity. At length, a horse whinnies loudly, a shrill noise in the hazy stillness. It rouses us out of our languor.

"Did Liam say how long he'd be gone?" Kat asks.

"A few days more at least." I run through different scenarios in my head. "Hopefully, only a few more, but I suppose it depends on what they encounter."

A fly buzzes around my head, one of many haunting the stable today. I swat it away, but another soon takes its place.

"Well, it should be quiet around here for a few days, at least with the princes gone and Emily departed," Puck says.

"How did that go, anyway?" Kat queries.

"Better than I expected. I was prepared for full on hysterics, but she was surprisingly subdued," Puck answers.

"Her hysterics seemed forced to me. Although, most of her behavior always has," I point out.

"What do you mean?" Kat asks.

"I mean, if something happened to Liam, I would be inconsolable. It would be as though a piece of me died with him. I don't even think I would have the strength to get out of bed and function every day, let alone go on a picnic."

"Yet, when I was growing up in Prescott, her family and Prince Stephan's were always very close. Maybe it brought her comfort to be with someone she has known all her life. People all mourn differently," Kat muses.

"Maybe," I mutter, unconvinced.

"Enough talk about death and such. Let's go put our feet in the water and try to find a more cheerful subject," Puck interjects.

We walk the short distance to a small stream which runs along the far reaches of the palace's land. It winds under a culvert to join a more robust cousin, before eventually flowing into the Crystal River. The three of us settle in a row along the banks, still soft and springy from the rain, our movement giving rise to an earthy scent. Birds flit from treetop to treetop, a jumble of songs. Cool water welcomes our feet, a pleasant haven from the domineering heat.

Puck grabs a few flat stones and skips them over the surface with ease. It is a trick I could never master, and he knows I envy his proficiency. "Have a try," he quips, holding one out to me.

I grasp the rock, try to hold it the way he has always shown me and angle my wrist just so. The stone flies over the water, bounces once, then sinks with a plop.

"Still can't do it, huh?" he quips.

"Be quiet," I exclaim, splashing him with my hands.

"Oh yeah?"

He leans into the stream with both arms and pushes a wall of water my way. Yet, I am too quick and roll out of the way just in time. The wave lands with full force on Kat, who looked up at the sun. She shrieks, standing up in the shin deep water, droplets pouring off her in a torrent. Puck and I freeze.

"Oh, my goodness, Kat, I'm so sorry…," Puck begins, but before he can finish, she kicks a giant plume of water at the two of us.

For a stunned second, we stand speechless before an all-out water fight breaks out. Arms and legs battle to see who can produce the biggest surge. The nearby birds fly off in alarm at the commotion. We hardly notice their escape as our laughter echoes across the stream.

When I return to my room, Madame Le Clare, who must have been listening for my return, barges out of her room. Her beady eyes survey my wet hair and bedraggled dress, a look of pure scorn flashes in her eyes. In my tenure at the castle, the headmistress and I have had a rather rocky relationship. At this point, we more or less politely ignore each other's existence. The fact that Liam and I are now courting forces her to be at the very least cordial and she does not mention my appearance.

"Good afternoon, Miss Olivia. Queen Helen wishes for you to stop by her chambers on your way to dinner."

"Of course, Madame. Thank you for letting me know."

She bows her head, then skirts past me with extra care, as if my disheveled state may somehow rub off on her.

Anne sits at her vanity in our room while Sadie coifs her hair. They both stare at me in surprise.

"Good gracious, Olivia. Are you all right?" my sister exclaims.

"Yes. Why do you ask?"

"Because you are soggy as a puppy left out in a storm. Have you been walking around the palace like that?"

"Umm, yes. Puck, Kat, and I had a bit of water fight at the stream."

While Sadie turns to hide a smile, Anne warns, "You really do need to remember others watch your example now. If you plan to be a future princess, you must behave in a more restrained manner."

My sister means well, and she is right. It is the aspect of being with Liam I am least fond of—life in a fishbowl where your every movement is a topic for discussion. "I know," I concede, "it was just a rough morning."

"What happened?" Anne asks with genuine concern.

While I explain about Becky, Sadie prepares me for dinner. She helps lift off my sodden dress, extraneous beads of water still dripping down my skin. Once dry, she helps me into a corset, followed by a dress of pale lavender, before getting to work on my hair. It is barely damp now and difficult to style. The maid starts one updo, but quickly abandons the plan and tries a different one.

"And when I got back here, Madame Le Clare told me the queen wants to speak with me before dinner." I finish my story.

At the mention of the meeting, Sadie works with renewed effort on my locks. She wants her handiwork well represented in front of the queen.

"Any idea what she could want?" Anne asks.

"No," I sigh, "likely just more about Liam and I and how to deal with the king."

"Try not to worry." My sister walks behind me and puts her arms around my shoulders. I see our reflections in the mirror, her vibrant mahogany hair next to my dull light brown. It still amazes me Liam even noticed me among all the more attractive ladies at court.

We depart down the stairs into a long corridor. Servants bustle past, some laden with trays, others with linens or papers, an orderly parade of worker ants, each secure in his purpose. At an intersection of hallways, my sister turns right while I continue on straight. A few more turns bring me to the wing, which houses the royal chambers. Two guards stand outside the queen's door. They move aside when I approach. My light knock brings Sally, the queen's personal attendant, to the door.

"Please come in, Miss Davenport. Her Highness expects you." She directs me to a chair in front of the unlit fire.

It is the same seat I took when the queen and I had a heart to heart discussion last winter. Then she had noted her desire for Liam and me to be allowed to marry. Though she has been my ally ever since, neither of us could have predicted the loss of Prince Harold.

Queen Helen emerges from another room. "Hello, Olivia."

"Your Highness," I say, dipping into a curtsey.

"Please sit," she instructs and settles across from me. "I just wanted to see how you were doing. I understand it was a sad morning for Becky Ryan."

"Yes, Your Highness," I whisper, afraid my emotions will get the better of me.

"It's always a tragedy, the loss of a child. Even an unborn one. I miscarried once."

"I'm so sorry," I exclaim.

"Yes, a year after Liam. I had just barely realized I was with child when it happened. I felt sure it was the daughter I always dreamed of having. But, alas, it was not meant to be." She sighs, a forlorn expression on her face.

"That must have been terribly difficult for you," I squeak out over the lump in my throat.

"Yes, but mothers must bear the pain with the joy. My boys brought me so much joy, so much fulfillment; I never felt anything missing after all."

She is silent for a moment, consumed by what is so obviously missing now. Her loss is so fresh—a grown son, her first—the pain must be unbearable.

"In any case," she continues, "I wanted to let you know I will do everything in my power to change the king's mind about allowing you and Liam to wed. All I ask is that you just be patient; let time soften the sharp edges of his pain. He did not have Harold marry for a strategic alliance so there is no reason to insist Liam does. I am sure my husband will realize this in time. He is a stubborn man and honestly has not been himself lately. I suppose none of us have."

"Of course, Your Highness," I say, but wonder how much time he will need since his majesty seemed quite adamant in his ruling. Yet, it does not matter how long—I would wait forever for Liam.

The queen rises and I am quickly on my feet to curtsey. She leads me across the room.

"I will see you in the dining hall in a few moments," she says, then slowly closes the door.

Anne and Kat sit at one end of a long trestle table, chatting amiably while they pick at their meals. I plop down next to Kat.

"Everything all right?" my sister asks.

"For now."

A servant lowers a plate of venison and vegetables in front of me. Steam rises from the hot fare, a tangle of savory aromas filling my nose. For the first time all day, I am hungry and eagerly lift my fork. Anne fills me in on some of the gossip from the day while Kat watches the door distractedly. Puck must have been held up at the stables. He usually joins us for at least a quick moment at the end of the dinner.

A herald announces the arrival of the king and queen. It is the first time they have dined in the hall since Harold's death. Everyone rises and bows. Once they are seated, people return to their meals. Conversations resume and soon a low hum fills the room. Different courtiers approach the royal couple's table to speak for brief periods. Finally, a sense of normalcy is restored and with it, a sense of relief. Only the Wolf Pack, who sit at the other end of our table, look despondent.

"They need a new ring leader. Up for the challenge?" I tease my sister.

"Thanks, but I'll pass. Maybe we could get them shipped down to Prescott so they can be with Emily and Jocelyn again," she suggests.

"Could we do that?" I ask excitedly.

"No," Anne laughs, the turns serious, "Olivia, now is your chance to become the leader. Try to sway them to your side. I am sure, given your status, they will want to come over. It would be a strategic move on your part. The more allies you have when you become a princess, the better."

As usual in court matters, my sister is right. This is my opportunity to establish a pecking order and a set of rules which are less based on vanity and cattiness. Besides, having all the ladies-in-waiting in my court could be helpful in the upcoming battle against the king.

"Would you ladies care to join us?" I call down to them.

Six heads bob up, then five immediately turn to Gretchen, who apparently holds the alpha role for the moment.

"Of course," she says.

They collect their plates and scoot down to our end of the table. Queen Helen, who has watched the exchange, grants me a quick smile, the leverage of their support not lost on her. For the next half hour, they fawn over me in a way which is both hysterical and uncomfortable, clearly ready to throw their lot in with whoever looks to be the highest-ranking female. Oddly enough, that is me—for now, at least, unless we can convince the king otherwise.

There is a commotion in the hallway outside, footsteps ringing on the stone floor and raised voices. A man barrels into the room at full speed, barely coming to a stop before the royal dais. Two guards leap down, swords drawn, until they recognize him as one of their own. It takes me a minute, but I finally place him as one of Prince Stephan's men who left with Liam. "Your Majesty, you must come at once to the stables. It is a matter of extreme urgency," the man gasps out through labored breaths.

"What is the meaning of this?" King William bellows, unused to being ordered anywhere. He rises to his feet, a commanding, regal presence.

"Your Majesty, there has been a terrible calamity—the prince has been killed."

My first thought is of Harold, whose death was clearly a horrible accident. Then, my heart freezes in my chest and time slows down. Voices now seem slow and distorted, hard to understand.

"What do you mean?" the king demands.

"I am truly sorry to inform Your Majesty; Prince Liam is dead. He was murdered."

"What? By who?" the monarch sputters and the queen collapses back into her chair.

The haze of my mind follows the conversation as though I watch a play being performed for someone else. Nothing could prepare me for the next words, which snap me back into reality like a sharp blow.

"By Sir Jack Davenport, Your Majesty."

After a collective gasp, an eerie silence fills the hall, every eye directed at King William. The queen has gone white. An attendant dutifully approaches her chair and puts a hand on her shoulder.

"I will find out for myself what is going on," the king declares. He pushes away from the table and heads for the door. Guards scurry into line behind him. The messenger hurriedly leads the way.

Queen Helen's and my eyes meet. In her stare, I see my disbelief and horror reflected. I rise and Anne puts a hand on my arm, but before she can say a word, I run out the door in the wake of the men.

My fast pace quickly closes the distance between the king's party and me. Deciding it is not worth it to draw unnecessary attention to myself, I deliberately remain a few steps behind. The stables are ablaze with torch lights, a glowing beacon just ahead, this unusual amount of activity explaining Puck's absence at dinner. Already, I can discern a crowd of men, their bodies silhouetted by the flames.

When we near them, Prince Stephan steps out from the pack to meet his quickly approaching uncle. "Oh, Your Majesty, thank goodness we have made it back to you. Your kingdom was almost lost—overthrown by this traitor."

He points and the crowd parts to reveal my father, bound and gagged, a man holding each elbow.

"Father!" I scream and run at him.

Heads whirl in my direction. A rough pair of hands seizes me before I can reach him. Despite my struggle, I cannot take another step. My father looks at me, a mixture of pain and fear in his eyes. His face swells with bruises and dry blood crusts the corners of the rag in his mouth.

"Nephew, have you gone mad?" King William demands. "Jack Davenport is one of my most trusted advisors. Explain yourself!"

"Of course, Your Majesty." He bows his head deferentially. "It seems raids in the north were nothing of the kind. An army was amassing—an army he was to command," again he points an accusatory finger. "He had spies rendezvous with him on our way up. But Prince Liam caught them meeting in the middle of the night. A fight ensued, which woke the rest of the company. We were finally able to subdue him while his conspirators got away. Sadly, this was not before Prince Liam was savagely murdered, along with his guard."

At the mention of Adam, something snaps in me. The panic and disbelief which filled me dissolve into rage. How could this man think anyone standing here would believe him?

"That is not possible," the king murmurs, echoing my exact thoughts. "Where is my son? If this murder took place, where is his body?"

"The men who got away took his body and dumped it in the river. They wanted no evidence left. Sire, we searched for hours, but could not find him. I am terribly sorry. A young soldier, Albert, was shot by a sniper and we decided to call off our recovery effort."

Prince Stephan's empathy sounds genuine. Men in the group nod their heads at the telling of the story. A few moved almost to tears. Yet, I still don't buy it. I know my father, what he is capable of. He would have died for Liam, who he had known since he was born.

"Ungag him this instant," the monarch orders. While they untie the gag, the King walks to his Master-of-Arms. "Jack, what has happened? Please tell me this is all a misunderstanding."

"Sire," my father rasps, "I do not remember what happened. I think my wine was drugged and I passed out. When I awoke, I was in chains. But I swear that I have never assembled an army with any intent to overthrow you."

"See there, nephew," the king notes, "there must be another explanation."

Prince Stephan sighs, looks at the ground, then meets his uncle's eyes. "Sadly, what I say is true. Ask the men. They will all attest to it."

King William looks questioningly at the soldiers. One by one, they nod in assent at the prince's claim, each gesture another stab wound to my heart. Sir Michael has arrived, along with Queen Helen, and a large contingent of others, who filter off into the darkness. The bulk of the court witnesses this condemnation of my father.

The king stands a long moment regarding the men. He turns to Sir Michael and barely whispers, "Take him away."

The knight nods to the two men who constrain my father and they lead him away. My father does not protest, but I stomp hard on the foot of the man restraining me. Upon release, I race to my father and throw my arms around his neck. Puck, who emerges from somewhere, grabs hold of my waist to pry me away, but not before I can whisper, "I will take care of this father. Trust me."

A horse nudges the top of my head from above. I lean against his stall door in the darkness, unsure where to go or what to do. The weak light of a candle floats in the air outside, where Puck paces. It advances toward me, the yellow halo of light expanding. My friend comes into view with Kat, her face distressed and tear stained. News spreads like wildfire through the palace. She runs to kneel at my side.

"This all must be a big mistake. Don't worry." She enfolds me in her arms.

I cannot find the words to answer her. My father's innocence is not in question with me, but it does not change the fact Liam is gone. I refuse to face the fact he is dead. I must find out what happened. I need answers.

Resolutely, I stand. "I need to speak to my father."

Puck and Kat look nervously from me to one another, but they do not stop me. Instead, each takes an arm to accompany me out of the stable. The night is warm, a muggy touch still lingering from the afternoon. A lone owl hoots, a mournful noise against the chirping crickets. Our mission leads us on less traveled paths and we must be careful of our footing in the dark.

Some minutes later, we arrive at the entrance of the citadel which houses the prison. Just picturing my father inside is enough to make me nauseous. As we mount the steps, two guards step from their posts to block our path. A ring of light surrounds them from sconces flanking the door. I recognize neither man. They must be from Prince Stephan's contingent.

"I am here to see my father," I state, my voice stronger than I feel inside.

"No one is allowed to see Sir Davenport," one man informs me.

"I demand to see my father now." I advance a step toward him. Puck and Kat stay behind.

The door rattles open and Sir Michael comes out onto the steps. His face is haggard, the usual bluster deflated as an empty waterskin. He regards me and my two friends for a moment. An inner struggle passes behind his eyes but flickers out too quickly.

"I am sorry, Olivia, but no one is permitted to see your father at the moment." His tone is kind, full of sympathy, so unlike any other time I've heard him speak.

He puts a steadying hand on my shoulder. There will be no arguing. Tears fill my eyes and I descend the stairs into the darkness. Puck and Kat walk me silently back to the palace.

Anne pops from her chair the moment I enter our room. Candles are lit on every surface, as though their brightness could help to drive away the bad news. She hurries over to me, her wet cheeks glinting in the flickering light.

"Oh, Olivia, this just can't be true. What are we going to do?"

I clasp her hands. "We are going to prove he is innocent, Anne."

"But, Liam..." her voice cracks and she trails off.

Until now, I used the outrage over the unjust accusations against my father to block out Liam, certain once the truth comes to light, it would explain his absence. Yet suddenly, before I can stop it, a tidal wave of panic crushes me. I sink to my knees, my sister lowering with me.

"I want to believe he isn't dead." My voice is a broken whisper. "But then, where is he? He would not just disappear. He could never do that to me or his father. Especially now. And Albert…"

It is this thought of Albert, a boy I grew up with, which breaks me. Not until this moment had I taken into account his failure to return with the company. Of course, it made perfect sense; he would have protected Liam with his life. What starts as a strangulated gasp quickly dissolves into sobs. Anne wraps her arms around my shoulders and rocks me back and forth, her weeping mirroring mine.

Focus and assess—I hear my father's words in my head, an expression he taught when I trained with the squires. I force all the hurt and anger from my heart. Tears will not help me. Now is the time for clear, concise thinking. My father needs me. And helping him will bring answers about Liam. If he is truly lost, I must make sure to not lose my father as well.

Breaking from my sister's embrace, I wipe my last tears. While we change into our nightclothes, I recount the evening's events to her, from the accusations at the stables, to my thwarted prison visit.

"In the morning, I will go to the queen. She will help me. I am sure of it."

We climb into our shared bed atop the covers in the warm room. An eerie silence fills the palace; even the nocturnal creatures are mute. In the silence, we both lie awake, neither wishing to voice the grave fears plaguing our brains. Eventually, the darkness overtakes me, and I fall into a fitful sleep.

Sometimes one awakens and for a moment does not recall the burden they fell asleep with. A blissful respite before the weight crashes back full force. This was not one of those times. From the second I open my eyes, I remember every last detail. My body is as heavy as my spirit, the night's rest seeming to have no effect. It takes all my effort to tamp down the wave of emotions waiting to break over me.

Faint light fills the sky when I part the curtains. It's barely dawn, too early to bother the queen, but not too early for Niobe. Hopefully, she will have some sound advice or, better yet, a premonition which could provide clarity. Suddenly, I remember her feeling of dread from yesterday. At the time, I had written it off as relating to Becky, but now it is clear, she felt a boding of what was to come.

The kitchen is just coming to life on my cut through to the healer's.

"Hello, Olivia," Mary says brightly. "It's too early for a sweet roll but help yourself to a peach."

My stomach is in no shape for food, not even the plump, juicy fruit in a basket on the counter. I thank her, a bit surprised at her cheeriness. She obviously has not heard the news. Perhaps they have tried to keep a lid on the details, a strategy which never seems to work.

Niobe sits head bent at the worktable when I enter. She rises to fold me in a hug, her frail figure almost ethereal in my arms.

"You knew," I whisper.

"Yes, I knew a misfortune was at hand, though I still have no clear sense of what happened or what will happen. I do not, however, believe one word about your father's involvement."

"Twenty men attested to his guilt," I bemoan, "Prince Stephan must have bribed them somehow."

My friend sighs and sinks down in an armchair by the unlit fire. "Yes, I feel much is amiss with the current story."

Whether someone told Niobe the full account, or she just knows, is anyone's guess. I had hoped she may have some answers, but now I must look elsewhere.

"I have to talk to the queen. She will help us sort this out. Will you come with me?"

"Of course, child. How distraught Helen must be— losing both her children within a month."

So whatever else Niobe thinks, she believes Liam is dead. And although there is no other likely explanation for his absence, my mind still rejects the idea. How could he be dead? How could he cease to exist without my heart feeling the loss at the exact moment? How can my life go on without him? Once again, I battle to keep my emotions at bay.

The healer rises, removes her apron and reaches for a shawl. Before I can help her wrap it around her shoulders, there is a rap on the door. It swings open to reveal three of the king's guards.

"Miss Davenport, you are to come with me immediately," the leader commands.

Thankful I may finally be able to speak with someone, I step forward, Niobe at my side.

"Not you, witch," he orders. "Only Miss Davenport."

"I will accompany her. I need to speak with King William myself," she says, her body drawn up in dignity.

"I am not here to escort her to His Majesty," the guard sneers. "I am here to escort her and her sister out of the palace."

At first, I do not comprehend what he means, but then dread sets in. Escort us from the palace? They banished us? I freeze.

He reaches to grab my arm, but Niobe admonishes him, "Just one second, lad, I will give my assistant a proper goodbye."

Once again, she pulls me into her arms and ever so softly whispers in my ear, "The orchard gate at dawn tomorrow."

It is all she can manage before hands pull me from her and the familiarity of the chamber. I nod to her as they drag me away. Servants stick their heads out of doors and windows to see the commotion. Confusion etches Mary's face when we pass the kitchen.

In our room, Anne quickly packs under the watchful eye of two more guards. Sadie tries to help, but is flustered by their presence. Opening my wardrobe, I stare at the colorful array of dresses. None of them will help me prove my father's innocence. In fact, I don't want anything at all from my belongings except for the necklace and the sword Liam gave to me as gifts, and a few notes of his, which I kept.

I toss these meager items into my trunk and lock it shut. Anne does not say a word, even when the lock on her last trunk clicks closed. We both hug Sadie, silent tears streaming down her cheeks. Then they escort us out a side entrance to a waiting carriage. Our luggage is tossed carelessly on the back and the door shut tight against us, as though we cannot be gone fast enough.

The ride to our old house is as surreal as the ride we took to the castle nine months ago. Worries, which seemed so immense then, are now trivial. Then, I had been terrified of the notion of living in the palace, but over time, the stone walls and corridors have become my home. There is no frame of reference without it, or Liam, or Niobe. Anne nervously twirls her engagement ring around her finger; her impending marriage now likely all but over. I cannot even find words to offer comfort and I will not waste my breath with false hope.

At length, we pull into the courtyard of our house, a cloud of dust engulfing the hooves of the horses. Mother opens the door, an anxious look of greater than normal proportions on her face. For the first time, she looks old. Lydia pushes her way out, her big blue eyes filled with bewilderment.

The driver reins the horses to a stop, drops our trunks on the ground. He yanks open the door and Anne and I spill into my mother's arms. Lydia runs over to join us. In a flash, the man is back in his seat, urging the horses away at a quick pace. Hoof beats fade into the distance, yet the four of us are loath to let go of each other. Lucy and Grace tiptoe out to take our trunks inside one at a time.

"Mother, what have you heard?" I ask when we draw apart.

"That your father has been imprisoned for treason and murder." Her words sound hollow.

Slowly, we make our way into the house and head for the sitting room. We each settle into a seat, a jumble of thoughts in our head. Lydia, unsure what to do or say, merely stands against the wall.

"I assume you two did not come home of your own volition?"

"No," I confirm. "We were escorted out this morning before I had a chance to speak with the king, the queen, or Father."

"What will become of us? We are disgraced," mother wails, balling a handkerchief in her hands.

For once, her theatrics are not overstated. If they find Father guilty, he will be executed, and his family exiled to the Mainland. The king would strip us of our titles, land, and fortune, and arrive there penniless.

Anne remains silent, still fussing with her ring. Grace and Lucy enter with a tray of tea and biscuits. Once pouring everyone a cup, they slink back into the kitchen. They would need to find employment with a new family after our downfall, a tough prospect since our dishonor will forever dog them.

"I know this isn't true. It is a setup. Olivia, you must get to the bottom of this," Mother states. Ironic, after all her years of disapproving and belittling my training, she immediately turns to me in times of trouble. "But, oh, I am so sorry about Liam. Your pain must be unbearable."

It should be, I suppose. Yet mercifully, something inside me has shut off, left numb. There will be a time to mourn Liam, but before I can let the grief consume me, I must save my father. Was it only yesterday I told my friends there was no way I could function without him? That anguish will come eventually, but for now I must stem its tide for the sake of my family.

"What do you plan to …"

A loud knock interrupts mother's question.

Now what?

Grace scurries to the front door and opens it a crack. Instantly, a man rushes inside with a frantic look on his face.

"Montgomery!" Anne exclaims, dashing into his open arms.

"Darling, I just heard. I got here as soon as I could."

"There is no future for us," my sister weeps. "Once your family finds out, they will demand you break the engagement."

"Never, my love. I will stand by you through this. That is where my place is."

After a morning of increasingly bad news, Montgomery's vow warms like a sliver of sunlight through dark clouds. Even Grace and Lucy, who have watched from the shadows, look relieved.

Mother rises to embrace him. "Thank you, my son, for your support."

We sit for a while discussing possibilities. My mother and our servants, who we insisted join us, show a keener understanding than I would have given them credit for. Talking to the king is paramount, but likely a lost cause. Access to father would be an even better option, at least he may be able to shed some much needed light on what transpired.

A commotion rings out in the courtyard.

"I'll go check," I sigh, not excited about the prospect of more drama.

Outside, about six squires mill about loading equipment on to some of our horses, who now bridled, are led from the barn. Seth, an old classmate of mine, oversees this operation. I march over to him.

"What is going on?"

"We are her to gather training supplies and horses and move them to the palace." He looks uncomfortably at his feet.

"The king already confiscates our things before there is even a trial?"

"This was by order of Prince Stephan," Seth mutters.

"Since when is he in charge?" I huff.

"Olivia, you know I have to follow orders, whether or not I agree with them. Word is that King William is too distraught to think clearly. Prince Stephan is making most of the decisions for him." At my look of pure disbelief, he moves closer and whispers, "I don't believe the charges, Olivia. They are unfathomable. If there is any way I can help you, I will."

My eyes fill with tears. He knows me, knows I will plan something. This offer could land Seth in prison. His belief in my father is a testament to the high regard in which his men hold him.

"Thank you," I barely manage, squeezing his hand, before I return to the house.

After a nearly uneaten dinner, I sit out in the kitchen garden. Many herbs are at their peak of pungency. Various scents waft across the air while the setting sun turns the sky orange. Crickets begin their merry night song. It reminds me of so many other times I sat on this bench to think. Never did I imagine the troubles I face tonight. Each passing hour increases the burden on my heart.

Lydia creeps out. For most of the afternoon, Ellen kept her busy in their bedroom, giving the adults time to come to terms with our situation. She is unusually quiet, not at all the vivacious five-year-old we all love. I wrap my arm around her, and she snuggles against my side. We sit in silence for a long time, the cricket's volume increasing in the newfound darkness.

Finally, she breaks the silence, "What they are saying about Father isn't true, right?"

"Right," I assure her, "It is all just a terrible misunderstanding. Our father would never kill someone like that."

"But if Father didn't kill Liam, who did?"

It is a question everyone has meticulously avoided. The obvious answer to me is Prince Stephan, a thought which is treason if uttered aloud. But why? And how could he get twenty men, some lifelong servants to my father, to go along with it? Maybe there was some kind of accident and for some reason, they needed to cover it up and blame a fall guy. It surprises me how analytically I can look at the situation. My heart still refuses to acknowledge the loss.

"I don't know," is my truthful answer to Lydia.

"You must be so sad, Livy."

"I am. But right now, I need to be strong. I need to figure out how to fix this."

"I know you can do it," she replies, gripping my hand tightly with her tiny fingers. "You always know how to fix things."

Her vote of confidence against this enormous obstacle adds to my resolve. "Come, let's get you to bed. I will need your help and I want you to have enough rest."

After tucking her in, I sit with my family in the sitting room. Despite a lot of theories and ideas, no one can contrive a way to gain access to either my father or the king. Exhausted by the events of the day and with no coherent plan to move forward with, I leave my mother with Anne and Montgomery and retire. Lydia still lies awake, although she has been in bed almost an hour.

Wearily, I change into some old nightclothes and motion my sister to move over. She makes room for me to climb into the bed beside her. Gently, she presses against me, her gold curls right under my nose.

"Don't worry, Livy," she whispers. "You are smart and brave and strong. You will make everything right again."

Kissing me on the cheek, she settles back down. In the darkness, ideas flit around my head, but no reasonable plan emerges. This, coupled with everyone's dependence on me, creates looming doubts. I hope my sister's faith in me is not misplaced.

Briefly, I doze in the wee hours of the night. At the first hint of light, I quietly dress, then head for the barn, grabbing an apple on my way through the kitchen. Most of the horses are gone, repossessed by the palace. An old nag named Minerva remains. She will have to do. I have her saddled in a few moments and head out our property's front gate.

Our journey is uneventful, through an old path in the woods. It is not as easy to traverse as the main road, but it keeps us out of sight. The air is heavy, but a slight breeze whispers among the trees. Minerva, for her part, seems happy to be out, her gait almost sprightly. We steer around some overgrowth, up a small rise and out into a thicket of holly bushes, where Niobe and I had picked ripe berries this past winter.

Tethering the animal to a tree, I reach in my pocket to retrieve the apple. "There you are, Minny. You wait here for me."

Her lead is long enough to reach some grass on one side and a nice patch of shade on the other. She should be fine here for a while. Slowly, I leave the cover of the grove, creeping toward the gate in the palace wall. I feel like a common thief, though I have done nothing wrong. When I arrive at the gate, I halt. Niobe gave me no instructions beyond meeting her here and I am hesitant to knock or call out. For a few long moments, I wait until the bolt on the other side of the gate squeaks out of its chamber. My friend's head pops out, relief flooding her face at the sight of me.

"Good girl," she praises, "now come."

I slink inside, Niobe sliding the bolt back into place while we both scan to see if anyone watches us. She holds out some garments to me—a dress, apron, and hat, which most palace servants wear. Quickly, I don the uniform, tucking every last strand of hair under the cap. Satisfied, my friend leads the way back to her chambers.

Once inside, she removes the rug from the trapdoor on her floor. It leads to her cellar, where she stores many herbs, baskets and books. Taking a lantern off a peg, I light it and we climb down the ladder.

"Now move the bookcase," Niobe instructs.

It swings open a secret door, revealing a hidden tunnel. The healer used this passageway last year to navigate the palace when she was under house arrest in her chambers. Just before we enter, she hands me a basket of fruit to carry. I accept it without question. Niobe guides me down several corridors, musty cobwebs the main décor, then up a rickety staircase, where each riser groans under my weight. A few more turns and she stops. In the wall, I barely discern the shape of a rectangle, before she pushes on it, sliding the hidden door to the side. We emerge behind a pillar in a marbled hallway. A familiar tapestry hangs on the wall across from us. It hangs near Queen Helen's chambers.

"Now, go down this hall and tell the guards the queen summoned this from the kitchen." She gestures to the basket of fruit.

Cautiously, I peek out from behind the pillar. No one is in sight, so I step into the corridor and walk to the queen's rooms. The plan is good, so long as the Queen Helen is in her room…and alone. My heart starts to pound. A guard posted outside barely acknowledges me when I stop in front of him. With a steadying breath, I say, "they instructed me to bring this from the kitchen for Her Highness."

He raps on the door. A maid opens the door a crack. "Ah yes, the fruit, at last. Come in."

Apparently, I was expected. The servant shuts the door behind me. After relieving me of the basket, she scurries out of the room. The queen sits in a window seat. She motions me over. Her face is tear-stained and her eyes weary. I curtsey and she rises to embrace me. "Niobe got you here, just as she promised."

"Your Highness, you must speak with King William on my behalf. My father would never have committed these terrible acts."

"I want to believe you, Olivia, but twenty men testified to it."

"Something doesn't add up. Prince Stephan framed him."

"That is a very serious accusation. One that would require iron clad proof. Do you have any?" Her tone is almost hopeful, she too needing a definitive answer.

"No. Not yet. But it would help if I could speak with my father. They will not allow me to. Please entreat the king to at least let me speak with him."

"King William is distraught. We have lost both our sons, his heirs. And now, he must face the fact one of his most trusted advisors, a friend, may have betrayed him. I will try to ask him, but he is not himself. Grief and anger cloud his thoughts and his judgment." Her green eyes fill with tears and she looks away, dabbing them with her handkerchief. "Prince Stephan is at his side every waking moment, making communication difficult."

"I have to do something to help my father. I can't lose everything." My voice trembles out the truth I do not want to admit.

"Stay in contact with Niobe. I will keep her informed. For now, you should go. It is dangerous for you to be here. If any guard sees you on palace grounds, they can arrest you on the charge of attempting to abet a traitor."

She embraces me again. I sigh defeat, then head for the door. Just before my hand reaches the lever, Queen Helen says sadly, "I am sorry for your loss, Olivia. I know you loved my son."

"I am sorry to you as well, Your Highness," I murmur from my curtsey. It is an inadequate consolation.

Back in the secret passage with Niobe, my head spins. It does not look as though the king and queen will be much help, at least not at the moment. I must find a way to speak with father. However, upon arrival at the cellar, no ideas on how to accomplish this present themselves.

The healer forces me to eat some light porridge, reminding me of the importance of keeping up my strength. She watches to make sure I empty the bowl. A full stomach helps me refocus on the task at hand.

"I am going to scout out the area by the prison to see if I can find out some information and maybe figure out a way to actually get to my father," I state.

"Just be careful, child," Niobe instructs, rubbing my back instinctively.

"I will."

The uniform provides the perfect cover. At Niobe's insistence, I carry a basket, a cloth over the top, to suggest some sort of business. In actuality, it is empty. Palace folk barely glance my way on the walk toward the stronghold. Servants are so commonplace, I blend right in. Again, I am reminded of words my father taught me: People usually see what they want to see. It is a ploy which has worked for me in the past.

There are two main entrances to the stronghold. One up the steps outside, where two guards stand sentry and one from an inner hallway, where I am certain two more guards stand. The only other entry is a small back door, used for prisoner release and deliveries. I have to circle around through some high brush to catch sight of it. Unfortunately, a man is stationed there as well. They are taking no chances. Gaining access to my father this way seems futile.

I steal back around to the primary thoroughfare and walk toward the palace. Perhaps, if I linger in the main halls, I will hear if they plan to bring my father before the king. Intercepting him somehow may be my only chance to speak to him. If courtiers are not talking, I can hopefully get some gossip out of a servant or two. It is not the best plan, but it is all I can come up with.

My steps are slow when I pass the church and the graveyard at its side. The sight of the royal tomb makes me pause. Will I have to endure Liam being laid out there? Not if they never find his body. A wall of grief slams into me and I try to regain my focus.

Two old women lay flowers at one of the markers. After a brief prayer, they shuffle to the gate. As they approach, one says, "So word is some ill fate has befallen Prince Liam. Though no one knows exactly what."

My ears perk up.

"I heard that Sir Jack Davenport murdered him," the other confides.

"A grab for power, I suppose. It always comes from the one you don't suspect," the first mutters sadly.

"Thank goodness Prince Stephan was there or who knows what may have happened next. But alas, poor Queen Helen. To lose both your sons. So tragic."

The other nods her head in sympathy. They continue to speak but are too far out of range for me to hear anything more. I almost follow them to see what else I can find out, but I see Prince Stephan himself hurrying in my direction. Panicked he will recognize me even in disguise; I hasten through the gate, across the small courtyard, and into the church to get out of sight.

It takes a moment for my eyes to adjust to the dimness. A quick scan around shows no one else is here. I clutch the edge of a pew and try to slow my thudding heart. But then I hear footsteps on the stairs outside. Could Prince Stephan have seen me? Did someone warn him I was on the castle grounds?

My eyes fly over the space, searching for a place to hide. The confessionals are the nearest suiable spot. It is a boxlike structure divided in two. A priest would sit on the side I choose, while the confessor would sit on the other. From that side, he can open a small latticework window to anonymously acknowledge his sins. I will myself to be quiet as my heart bangs against my chest. There is also latticework on the top half of my side. Though the holes are small and hard to see through, I duck down below it.

The church door creaks open, brightening the crack between the door and floor of the confessional an instant before banging shut. His steps echo on the flagstone up the center aisle, then down again, then back up. Ever so slowly, I lift my head up and press an eye against one perforation in the door.

Prince Stephan paces, hands running through his hair in an agitated manner. After a moment, his eyes fall to the right of the confessional where a bank of candles stands below a statue of the risen Christ. He staggers over to them in obvious distress. I feel ashamed to secretly witness his personal grief. The deaths of his cousins affected him more than I had thought. His drawn face and heavy eyes tell the story of torment.

From my angle, I can barely make out the profile of his body. Kneeling, he takes a long stick, ignites it on an already glowing candle, then lights a new one. The prince bows his head in prayer.

"Forgive me," he says, his whispered tone echoing in the empty space, "forgive me for what I have done."

The hair on the back of my neck stands up. Every fiber of my being leans toward him to hear the next words.

"It is a sin. I confess this and I am sorry. Yet I know I will be spared eternal damnation because I spared him."

Somewhere in the recesses of my mind, I am brought back to the dais where Lord Otto lies dead and Niobe fights for her life. And Brother Alastair, the self-righteous friar, blustered about eternal damnation if one murdered a royal.

"It was the only way for this to work," the prince continues. "I have sinned, but I will make you proud. I will be a just and kind leader. I trust you will grant me the mercy which I have granted him."

As abruptly as he entered, he rises, straightens his doublet, pats down his hair and walks calmly out, the door clicking shut behind him.

Collapsing onto the floor in the stall, I steady my breathing. It all makes perfect sense now. Prince Stephan plans to take over the kingdom. With his two cousins gone, he is next in line for the throne. Why did I not see this before?

But I cannot even concentrate on this, because his words brought into reality what my heart always knew—Liam is alive.

81

Liam

A rough hand shakes him awake. "Prince Stephan has important news. Come with me."

He rubs the sleep from his eyes, rising from his bedroll and exits the tent. Adam is right behind him. The sun is about to rise, remnants of the dark night still clinging to the landscape. The man disappears into the brush. When Adam gives him a quizzical look, he shrugs and follows. No one stirs in the camp. On the way, the only person they see is Albert, who relieves himself by a tree.

Prince Stephan waits in a small clearing, a handful of men at his side. He looks grave. Perhaps a scout has brought some bad news from the north.

"I'm sorry to do this," his cousin states.

Suddenly, men draw swords from all sides. They point directly at him. Adam cries out in protest, reaching for his weapon. Before he can unsheathe it, the man behind him shoves his sword right through the guard's back. When he withdraws it, Adam falls to the ground, lifeless.

The treachery becomes clear to him now, and he reaches for his own dagger. They grab his arms and he struggles mightily. There is yelling from behind and Albert bounds out of the woods, sword in the air, running to his prince's aid. A burly man makes short work of the boy.

Despite his own resistance, he is overpowered, too outnumbered to have ever had a chance. In one last act of desperation, he tugs at the fabric of his already torn sash. A piece of the bright red fabric comes free in his hand. He stuffs it into the leaves of a passing bush while they wrestle him from the clearing.

"Take him to the designated place," Stephan orders some, then to others says, "and bury the bodies."

Mouth gagged, they tie his wrists in ropes and bind it to the saddle of a horse. With two men in front of him and two men behind him, they set out at a brisk pace in the wakening dawn. For hours, they ride with no respite. Night falls, the sky dimming with each moment. The bindings chafe at his wrists, a constant dull ache. His legs burn from squeezing them for so long to retain his balance on the horse. Beads of sweat roll down his face, but he cannot wipe them away. Surely, they will have to stop once darkness takes over.

A man in the front of the group holds his hand up and the caravan halts.

"Here for the night," is the only order he utters.

The man dismounts, along with four others. They will let him off now. Perhaps there will be a chance to escape when they untie him. Yanked from the saddle, he is thrown to the ground. A hard kick to his mid-section dispels any thoughts of trying to run. Prince Stephan's men mean business, and all have their guard up. They tie him to a tree, ropes so tight it constricts his breathing. Around a small fire, they eat a scant meal. None is offered to him, merely a quick sip of water too warm to be refreshing.

Scenes of the early morning struggle play out in his mind. The initial confusion felt when they surrounded him and Adam. Horror at the sight of Adam cut down so cruelly, with no way to help him. And Albert, the poor young boy, trying to defend his prince against such a heinous attack. Both now dead. Both shoved like an afterthought into a cold, shallow grave.

Prince Stephan would reach Adelina tonight. What tale would he tell? Endless ideas plague his mind. All afternoon he had imagined the many false stories which may come from his cousin's lips. His father is in danger. His kingdom is in danger.

He strains against his bonds, the gag pulling tighter across his already dry mouth. A moan escapes. "Shut it," one man warns, but they do not spare him a glance.

His head lolls to his shoulder where his ripped sash dangles. A clue for his rescuers…if any come.

Olivia.

Her image flashes before him. She will come. He must believe this. It is the only hope to sustain him right now. Exhaustion takes hold and he sleeps, her face the last thing he remembers.

84

For a long while, I sit on the floor of the confessional, knees pulled up to my chin. The truth itself is not enough. I need proof and I need to get it fast, before Prince Stephan realizes I am on to him. Somehow, I have to find Liam, prove he is alive, and his cousin's story is a lie.

The momentary comfort of knowing my fiancé lives is quickly replaced with worry. Where is he? Is he injured? Does he try to make his way back to me? Will he think I believe he is gone and move on? Certainly, he must know me better than that.

Finally, I rise, my back seizing up in protest and make my way back to Niobe's. It is past midday, the sun just beginning its descending arc to the west. Courtiers, servants and villages mill about, tending to late afternoon duties. I keep my head down and walk with purpose, the basket clutched around my elbow. At the healer's, I can barely get the story out fast enough.

"There, my girl. I knew he wasn't dead. My heart told me just as yours did." She squeezes my hand.

"Yes, it is good news, but it doesn't change the fact Liam is still missing and my father may be charged with murder. I must see Father somehow. I will wait until nightfall and see what I can do."

Niobe fixes me a plate of fruit, cheese, and bread. For months after her recovery, I have been taking care of her. Our roles now reversed. My mind races with a thousand thoughts, a mental madhouse in my brain. *Focus and assess.* Father's words never rang truer.

The healer quietly prepares some tinctures and poultices to distribute to servants in the village, a task I would normally help her with. Methodically, she removes flasks from the overcrowded shelves about the workbench and mixes them into vials. Watching her perform this everyday routine, I relax and a plan forms in my brain. One riddled with many flaws, as so many are in their infancy. I will need to ruminate on it to iron it out.

"Niobe," I say, after a bit, "could you get someone you trust from the village to deliver a message to Puck for me?"

"Yes," she answers simply and shuffles to the cabinet on the right of the workbench, from which she produces paper, an inkpot, and a quill.

Hastily, I jot down:

Meet me where you tried to teach me again what I still cannot master. Be there tonight at 9.

There is no need to sign it. My oldest friend will know my handwriting. I fold the paper into quarters. Niobe hides it among the remedies in her basket. With a consoling pat on my arm, she heads out the door.

All afternoon, I wait in the healer's rooms. Though it's stuffy, I dare not open the door. Full of nervous energy, I recline onto her bed hoping to calm my mind. Instead of thoughts about how to gain access to my father, tears come unbidden, tears of sadness, but also tears of relief. Liam is alive. Even though I would not yet allow myself to grieve at his passing, the knowledge had pressed on me like a pile of stones. Once lifted, the dam has broken, and I weep freely.

A life where I cannot be with Liam is unimaginable enough, a life where he ceased to exist would be unbearable.

I must doze for a while, because the next thing I know, Niobe shakes me awake. Sleepily, I stumble back into her front room where a covered tray is set on a small side table. She lifts the lid to reveal a roasted chicken with some green beans and potatoes. The smell of it makes my stomach grumble.

"I can't eat your dinner," I protest. "You need it to regain your strength."

"No, child, you will need it. Hard days lie ahead of you. Besides, I barely eat what they send me each night anyway."

"Thank you." I say. "Did you hear anything useful in the village?"

"Not especially," she replies. She takes some cheese and bread from a cupboard and joins me. "They know your father was arrested for suspected treason, but no one believes Prince Liam is missing. They think stories of his death are an exaggeration. Some say he and King William try to decide how to punish your father and so they remain out of sight."

It's probably better that way. The kingdom may not be able to withstand the turmoil of losing another prince right on the heels of the first.

"Do you think it would help if I tried to talk to William? Tell him what you've overheard?" Niobe asks. Her relationship with the king dates back to his childhood. She could likely gain access to him.

"No. I need proof. Without it, it is only my word against Prince Stephan and the twenty men he somehow must have bribed into going along with his story."

The clock on the mantle chimes the seven o'clock hour. Two more hours left until I meet Puck. They drag on eternally. At first, I try to help prepare some remedies for tomorrow, but I cannot concentrate. Mostly, I sit on a stool, my foot tapping furiously, as I check the clock every three seconds.

Finally, a little before nine, I bid Niobe farewell. She places a small basket in my hands, which contains a few bandages, a few healing salves, and some herbs for a fever. Though I have not spoken about my plan, she still seems to know inherently what I will do. For a long moment, she embraces me at the door, then wordlessly kisses my cheek before letting me out into the night.

Skirting through the outer recesses of the village, I walk to the stream. Was it only two days ago I sat there laughing with my friends? When I reach the banks, Puck steps out from behind some large juniper bushes.

"Livy, what happened?" he whispers. "Were you banished from the palace?"

"Yes, and I cannot gain access to my father or the king." We creep back to the cover of the bushes.

"What is going on?" In disbelief, he listens as I explain the events from yesterday morning until now. "Are you sure that is what Prince Stephan said?"

"Yes, Puck, I am sure. I have to figure out some way to see my father. I am going to the prison now. There has to be a way."

"I'll come with you."

We creep away from the stream and through some rough grassland which lies behind the prison tower. The small back door looms in front of us. It is likely my best chance at entry. A figure stands sentry outside, his outline visible against weak light from a single sconce.

"Will you go see who that is for me?"

Puck nods. He heads over to a hilly path and walks down to the door. He startles the guard at first, but then they converse. After a second, the sentry opens the door and says something. A larger figure appears from the shadows. They all share a brief exchange before Puck hurries back up to me.

"It was Seth. I asked if I could see your father. He said no visitors were allowed. I begged him, for your sake, then he called for Sir Michael, who pretty much just chased me away."

For a moment, I ponder the situation. There is no more time to wait. Smoothing out my servant's dress and tucking loose strands of hair into my cap, I walk determinedly down to where the two men continue to talk. They stop mid sentence, confused looks on their faces.

"Sir Michael, it is me, Olivia Davenport," Better to be up front about things.

A brief look of surprise flashes in his eyes, but he quickly turns serious. "Olivia, you shouldn't be here. Technically, I could arrest you. For everyone's sake, please go home right now."

"I can't do that," I answer, while Seth's head volleys between me and his superior.

"Olivia, please do not make things any worse for your family," he entreats.

"Do you think my father did what they claim?"

"Twenty men attested to it."

"That is not what I asked you."

"Prince Stephan has given his account."

"That is *not* what I asked you," I interrupt forcefully. "Do you think my father did what they claim? For goodness sake, Sir Michael, you have known him for decades."

He is quiet for a long moment, then barely whispers, "No. I do not believe it."

"Nor do I. So, I need to talk to him and see if he can remember anything which could be helpful in proving his innocence."

"I can't allow that," he replies, yet his usual gruffness is gone.

"I know we have had our differences in the past." A kind way to describe our contentious relationship. "But I beg you, please help me now. It is not only my father's future you could change, but the future of the kingdom."

Seth's eyes are as wide as saucers. Sir Michael stares over my head into the darkness. Puck materializes by my side, puts a hand on my shoulder. This is it, my only chance to see my father. The air fills with a palpable attentiveness while we await his answer.

"Wait here," he finally instructs and disappears into the prison.

After several tension filled minutes, the door cracks open. "Come on, Olivia," he orders. "You two stay here."

The entry shuts behind me and my eyes adjust to the dim light of a vestibule. Sir Michael takes my arm to guide me forward along a short hallway, then two left turns, to a staircase which spirals up out of sight.

"It is the first door at the top of the stairs. I sent the guard on an errand. He will be back within twenty minutes, so you have ten."

Like lightning, I am up the stairs to the first door on a small landing. It is solid wood but for a small square opening at eye level covered with bars. I press my face against to cold, unforgiving iron.

"Father?" I whisper.

"Olivia?" he says softly back. "Is that you?"

"Yes. I am here, Father."

Next thing I know, his face is opposite mine. I reach through the bars to touch his cheek.

"You are so warm. Do you have a fever?"

"I think so, but that is not important now. How did you get in here?" While he asks, I rummage through the basket Niobe gave me. I had forgotten it was in my arms the whole time.

"Sir Michael. He believes in your innocence. Here," I produce a small vial. "Take this. Hopefully it will help with your fever."

He quickly sips the contents and hands the empty container back to me. I drop it unconsciously into the basket. My mind races with all we need to cover.

"I don't have much time. Father, I know Prince Stephan is lying. I overheard him in the church when he thought he was alone. Liam is still alive. I need to find him to prove you didn't do what they said. Is there anything, any detail, you can remember that could help me?"

"We left here and camped the night about halfway to Lindenwood. Do you remember where we stopped last fall?"

I nod.

"We ate and I suddenly felt incredibly drowsy and I went to sleep. When I awoke, Prince Liam was gone, and they accused me of killing him and dumping his body in the river. They must have drugged my ale so they could carry out their plan. They bound me up. I tried to fight back, but to no avail."

This explains the bruises on his face. Now, he looks at me through eyes which are red-rimmed and glassy. Framed by his matted hair and many days' worth of growth fill his jaw.

"Are they feeding you?"

"Not much."

I reach to feel his cheek once more. "You are feverish. The remedy I gave you will not help you for long. You must ask for the king's physician or Niobe."

"I have. They will let me see no one. Prince Stephan pushes for my execution."

A pit forms in my stomach. My father will only get worse if untreated. With a fever and inadequate nourishment, nature may win out before the executioner has his chance.

"Olivia, go now before they catch you. I would tell you to not to risk your freedom and your life to save me, but I know you are your father's daughter." Tears fill both our eyes. "I love you, my sweet girl."

"I love you too, Father. I will prove your innocence. I promise."

With a squeeze of our hands through the bars, I duck back down the stairs. Sir Michael smiles sadly when I thank him and lets me back out the door. Puck waits with Seth, who hugs me tightly and repeats his vow to help if he can. When we head to the gate in the castle wall where I entered so many hours ago, I explain my plan to Puck and what I need him to do for me.

"Tell Niobe I left for the night." I instruct just before he shuts the gate. "I'll see you in the morning."

Poor Minerva stands forlornly by the tree where I left her. She is happy to see me and happier still once home in the safety of her stall. I spend a moment brushing her down. When I find a carrot for her, she whinnies in appreciation.

When I walk into the house, a glow emanates from the kitchen. My mother, Lucy, and Grace all murmur to one another. They deserve an explanation of what I learned, even though it will put them in danger. Yet, before speaking to them, I go to my room.

Lydia lies in bed asleep, a tiny figure on the large mattress. Her golden curls frame her face in the crack of light from the hallway. Next door, the room is where Ellen sleeps is dark. Quietly, I enter the bedroom, open my trunk, and pull out a small leather pouch. When the string loosens, I dump a small rock into my hand, the  symbol barely visible in the dim room.

It is time to go see Athos.

Holding the stone brings me a measure of comfort. When Athos gave it to me, he promised I could use it to find him if I was ever in need of his help. King William has looked the other way since the outlaw saved his life, which hopefully means he is still in Stewartsland. Now I need him to save both Liam and my father.

When I enter the kitchen, my mother, Grace, and Lucy look up from their huddled mass at the counter. They look as tired as I feel. Lucy comes over to wrap me in an embrace.

"We were worried about you," she sniffles, dabbing the corner of her eyes with a napkin. "We don't need you in trouble as well."

"I saw Father," I say, looking directly at my mother.

For someone given the theatrical emotion, she is amazingly calm, perhaps overwhelmed by the seriousness of the situation. "Is he all right? Are they taking care of him?"

"Barely." I stand across from her. "He did not do this. We all know. I have a pretty good idea of what is going on, but for your own safety, I can't tell you. All I can say is I am leaving again in the morning. What I plan to do is grounds for treason. They could come for all of you if they suspect you helped me in any way. You all need to understand that."

Mother reaches over the counter and takes my hands, a rare supportive gesture. "There is no one else I would trust to save him, Olivia. No one. Please promise me you will be careful."

After all her years of disparaging my training, all the fights, all the hurt feelings, this statement may be the most touching words she has ever said to me.

"I will be. I will make everything right again."

None of them ask for further explanation, they simply help me prepare. Grace and Lucy pack food which travels well—dried meat strips, hard cheese and dried fruit. Mother brings me some flint and a compass, items which belong to my father. I also have the medicines and bandages from Niobe. In the barn, I find an old saddle bag. There is also a worn leather jerkin left behind by the squires because of its ragged condition. It is big, but it will do. This and a couple of filled water-skins round out my supplies.

Around midnight, we retire after long, silent hugs from all three, each fraught with anxiety and faith. Lydia curls her small body into mine when I lie down next to her. Her sleeping breath fills the room with a calming cadence for my overtaxed mind. I concentrate on its innocence and purity until I finally doze.

Pale light seeps into the room around the curtain's edges when I wake. Softly, I slip out of bed, still in my servant's dress, now wrinkled. In the corner are the boots from my training days, which glide onto my feet like long-lost friends. For a long minute, I watch Lydia sleep, then gently kiss her tiny cheek. She does not stir.

In the kitchen, my gear stands ready. Besides the filled saddle bags and the jerkin, there is a small dagger given to me by my father some years ago, and a sword given to me by Liam only a few months past. Gathering everything up, I head for the barn.

Minerva mildly protests when I put all my belongings on her back. At her advanced age, it would be unfair to expect her to carry me as well. I lead her out of my family's gate and through the back fields and forest to the hemlock grove. The dawn air is warm, but a light breeze makes it more pleasant. Birds flutter and chirp in the sky, eager to stretch their wings before the oppressive afternoon heat sets in. My horse slowly trots along, tail swishing in time.

Puck waits just inside the tree line. Relief fills me at the sight of him. Although I trust him implicitly, my plan hinges on him doing what I asked without getting caught. So far, so good. However, as I approach, I notice another figure with him and not one, but two horses from the royal stable. The other's face is familiar. It is Franklin, Sadie's beau, who helped me out last year when I unraveled the conspiracy against the king.

"Good morning," Puck says brightly.

"I don't think you understood my instructions," I state, stopping in front of them.

"Oh, I understood perfectly. I just altered them a bit."

"Puck, you can't come with me. You just can't," I bluster. "It's too dangerous. It's treason. And now you have involved poor Franklin."

The young man steps forward. "I am only here to bring your mare home."

"That was supposed to be Puck's job," I chide.

"I'm sorry, Livy," exclaims my friend, "but I will not let you go off on this quest alone. If you try to thwart me, I will sneak after you. I believe you are well versed in people sneaking on missions."

Any arguing would be pointless. Puck is not nearly as stubborn as I, but when he decides something is important, that is that. Half of me is thankful to have a companion, but the other half despairs over the peril he puts himself in. Kat will be beside herself when she discovers he is gone.

"Very well," I concede, then turn to Franklin. "I don't know how much you know about where we intend to go and what we intend to do. I truly hope no suspicion arises that you assisted us. Please be careful."

"I will be. Honestly, no one really pays me much mind in the castle, so I wouldn't worry. Oh, and I brought you these." He extends his arms to reveal a man's shirt and pants. "They may be a little big."

"Thank you, Franklin. They are perfect."

I skirt behind some overgrown and change from my servant's dress into my new outfit. Then, I braid my hair. They are simple things, an outfit and a hairstyle, but they remind me of all my years of training. How I have missed this part of my life. It is invigorating to have it all brought back.

"I'm not sure what to do with this," I wonder, emerging with the dress in hand.

"I'll take it to your house with the horse," the boy offers.

"Thank you, Franklin, for everything."

At my embrace, he falters, and returns it with awkward arms. Then, he takes Minerva's lead, wishes us well, and strikes off on the path toward my home.

"So, where to?" Puck's tone is light in an effort to relieve any tension.

"To the last place my father remembers. It should take most of the day to get there. We must hasten. When they realize I am gone, and now you as well, someone will surely be hot on our tail."

"Once we get there, then what?"

"Then we find Athos."

"How?"

"No idea."

"I was afraid you were going to say that."

We mount up on two geldings, which are eager to be off. A rising sun burns off the morning haze. Today looks to be hot again. Our road at this early hour is fairly empty and we set out at a brisk pace. Several merchants pass us in the opposite direction, their wares piled on carts headed for the marketplace. Here and there, a farmer crosses our path, one herding sheep across the road. The farther we get from the city, the fewer people we see.

I have not been out here since I snuck on the mission last fall. Circumstances were so different then. At that time, my biggest problem was my mother, who was adamant my training should end. The mission seemed my only chance to prove what I wanted out of life. Then, I met Liam. There was a connection with him from the start. He made me believe in a life without my training, but his father has quashed any hope of this when he broke our engagement.

We stop mid-day next to a creek for a hurried meal. Birds flit about us noisily, hoping for some crumbs. The horses refresh themselves with a drink while we sit in the shade of a large oak.

"How long before someone comes after us?" Puck asks, the juice of a peach running down his chin. He wipes it on his sleeve.

"As soon as they piece together we are gone, which will most likely be later today. We have to keep moving."

I rise and dust off my breeches. It feels good to be back in simple clothes, no corsets or uncomfortable dresses. A dragonfly darts around my head, its jewel-like body glistening in the sun. My friend follows wordlessly to the horses. We saddle up and are off again.

In the late afternoon, we arrive at the place where the men camped on the night things went bad for my father. I am pleased we have made such good time. There are signs of recent use—a ring of stones filled with ashes, scuffs of boot prints, and a discarded piece of leather from a broken horse's bridle.

While Puck ties up the horses, I put my tracking skills to work. This was a specialty of mine when I trained. Trampled leaves, bent twigs, and disrupted earth, all provide evidence which can tell a tale of what occurred. After a cursory examination of the site, I walk over to my friend.

"I can see two different directions where men walked. This one," I point right, "goes down by the stream. It is the more heavily used of the two. But this one," I gesture left, "is much less used. Let's follow it."

Puck double checks the ropes on the horses, then joins me. We inch slowly along the trail checking for clues. It is not exactly an overgrown area, though clearly not used often. There is no dirt to leave footprints, only crushed plants and broken stems, which try mightily to straighten back up toward the sun.

"See this?" I motion at the affected area. "These markings are a few days old."

We progress at a snail's pace, stopping at times for me to inspect a new spot of interest. At length, we emerge into a sizable clearing. Here it becomes harder for me to tell which way to go. Two fairly well traveled paths diverge in opposite directions. I edge down one, my eyes scanning for any kind of hint. Just when I am about to give up and go search the other path, something catches my eye. On shaky feet, I walk to a bush where a crimson piece of fabric clings to the branches. With a sturdy tug, a sash floats out into my hands. Puck rushes up behind me.

"It's Liam's," my voice is barely audible.

"That's good, right? It means we are headed the right way."

"Yes," I murmur. Somehow the sash solidifies Liam's absence, sets my mind reeling in a whirlwind of fear.

"Let me go back and get the horses," Puck suggests. "I'll bring them to the clearing, and we can decide what to do, stop for the night or continue on farther."

I nod distractedly and he heads back. It will not be easy to lead both horses through the brush alone, but I cannot find the wherewithal to go help him. Instead, I sink to my knees, my fingers running nervous waves over the smooth, satin material, particularly around the ragged edges where it ripped apart. There was a struggle. Liam did not go willingly.

The immediate area around the bush shows significant damage to the foliage and earth. I had been so focused on Liam being alive, thoughts of him being captured and imprisoned only skulked around the outskirts of my mind. Until now.

Where was he? Was he cold? Hungry? Injured? Did Price Stephan care if he died or not? Horrible images flash through my mind and I grasp the sash tighter, even as rocks dig into my lower legs.

It takes all my determination to rise. Of all times, this is the time to focus. Straightening my jerkin, I step back toward the clearing when Puck's voice fills the air. It is still far off, but I hear him clearly.

"I have nothing of value. I swear it. Please, just let me be on my way."

In a flash, I am off in his direction, hand already reaching for the hilt of my dagger. Up ahead I can make out Puck between our two horses, where two men accost him. They hear my approach and turn.

"Leave him alone," I yell. Rather than cower in fear, they stand bewildered by my appearance.

"I already tried that," my friend states.

"Please," I entreat, now standing in front of them, "I have something in my bag to show you."

Hopefully, they will let me get the stone out. If they recognize it, our connection to Athos may be enough to scare them away. They let me push past them to access my saddle bag, where I rummage amongst my belongings.

"Truly, we have nothing of value." Puck asserts.

"Oh, I wouldn't say that," a familiar voice drawls from behind us.

My shoulders sag in relief when a sprightly man steps out from a cluster of trees.

"I was wondering when you would get here, Olivia."

I drop the flap closed on my saddle bag and run right into the open arms of Athos.

While Athos and I embrace, several more men step from the woods. Puck receives handshakes and relaxes at our turn in fortune. I should have known it would not be necessary to find Athos. He found us.

"It would be best if we could get out of sight," he suggests.

We hike off the path into the forest, the men carefully guiding our horses over the rough terrain. The canopy of trees blocks out a good deal of the sun, but the outlaws are so familiar with the area, they could find their way in the dark.

"Athos, this is Puck," I introduce when my friend joins us at the head of the group.

"Nice to meet you. Didn't leave him behind again, Olivia?" Athos teases, knowing I snuck on the Lindenwood mission last fall in Puck's place.

"No," I laugh. "He was too smart for that this time."

A large tree trunk lies across our path. Puck and I hurdle it easily, but Athos is slower to get over it.

"How is your leg?" I question. In the spring, one of Athos' men came to the castle seeking medicine for the grave wound.

"Almost as good as you new, thanks to your help." He smiles, even as a flash of pain crosses his face.

"After everything you did to help save the king and my father, I am still the one who owes you thanks," I say. "And now, I must ask for your help again."

"Yes," he muses, "I've been expecting you. When we arrive at camp, we can talk."

It is slow going for a time, the dense foliage hard to navigate. Eventually, the trees spread out and we mount a small rise. Hollowed out like a bowl, the middle is filled with pine trees, clustered throughout like a small army. We descend over the rim into a well-hidden dell.

Our horses are led off in one direction, while we follow Athos in the other. They have cut lower bows from the trees to create a wide lane. In the middle of the dell, there is a small clearing where Athos has set up camp. Men wander in and out through other paths cut into the trees. Some clean their gear, a few sway in hammocks, and one whittles a bear out of a chunky stick. A shock of gray hair catches my eye over by the unlit campfire.

"Hello, Claude," I say to the beloved cook.

"Hello, mi'lady. So good to see you. In trouble again, are we?"

"As always," I kid.

We chat amiably for a few moments before I join Athos, who sits with Puck in a makeshift headquarters. One large piece of fabric stretches above an old wooden table and some mismatched chairs. A dilapidated trunk stands, its lid open, maps, a compass, some lanterns and one shiny dagger hilt all visible inside.

I plop in a chair directly across from Athos and blurt, "Liam has gone missing and there are rumors of his murder. What do you know?" Puck and I lean forward in anticipation.

"About a week ago," Athos begins, "a small contingent of men and I were returning from an excursion in the west. We came upon signs of a struggle and two freshly dug graves."

"Are they nearby?" I interrupt. "You must take me to them."

He holds up his hands for me to wait and continues, "It was an unusual scene because there clearly were a number of men. Most, it seems, returned south, but a much smaller party continued north. Normally, we would have kept to our own business, but they hastily buried one of the bodies. A hand still protruded from the ground—a hand wearing this."

He reaches into his pocket and produces the ring of service worn by Adam. I blanch at the sight of it, my stomach dropping. Though I thought Adam was most likely dead, it is chilling to see this memento of him.

"I see you know to whom this belongs," Athos states.

"Yes. It belongs to Prince Liam's personal guard."

"Knowing this," which of course Athos did, "we exhumed the other body to see if it was Prince Liam. It turned out to be a young boy. Tall and thin with dark hair. I take it from your expression you know who it was."

Albert.

My heart breaks at the vision of his life taken so cruelly. All I can manage is a nod. My voice swept away in a torrent of sadness. Puck puts a hand on my shoulder.

"We didn't quite understand what had occurred, and were wary considering the death of Prince Harold," Athos goes on, "so we set up a watch on the area. If Liam is missing now, my guess would be he was in the party which headed north."

"Yes," I mumble

"Odd that you and your friend are the only ones who search for a missing crown prince. One would think the king himself would be out searching for his son. And yet, you two sneak about the task as if you were criminals."

"Well, the king thinks Liam was murdered."

"Who exactly do they accuse of this crime?"

"My father," I answer flatly.

Athos' eyes widen in disbelief. "That cannot be."

"Twenty men confirm Prince Stephan's story."

"Clearly they were bought. There is no man more loyal to the king than Jack."

"Tell that to King William," I grunt.

"I am surprised to hear he even considered it."

"He is still grief-stricken over Prince Harold's death and isn't thinking clearly. The loss of his other son hit him hard. I hear he has been locked away in near seclusion," Puck adds.

"So, you think this is all some coup planned by Prince Stephan?" Athos surmises. "Why leave Liam alive then? He may as well have killed him since he had all those men bought to confirm his story."

"He was worried about eternal damnation."

"About what?" Athos asks.

"Father Alastair said last year any man who would murder royal blood will suffer such a fate."

An image of the self-righteous friar surfaces. While Lord Otto, the king's half-brother, lay dead at our feet, he told Prince Stephan the lifeless man would be spared eternal damnation since the prince killed him before he could kill King William. Otto seemed about to reveal his accomplices when Stephan had silenced him with a knife to the chest. When Prince Stephan had blanched at Father Alastair's words, I had chalked it up to his cowardly nature, but now I wonder if he was frightened by the friar's decree.

This would explain why he spared Liam's life. Yet, it also sparks an idea in my mind. Lord Otto's motives were always unclear. First, he tried to usurp Lindenwood to trap King William and then he attempted outright murder. Challenging a popular king with a powerful army had guaranteed him almost no chance of success. There had been a mysterious "she" who had helped him, but surely this alone would not have increased his odds. However, if he was in collusion with Prince Stephan all along…

"You have that most pensive look I came to admire, Olivia. What are you thinking?" the bandit asks me.

"Have you heard of any recent activity near Lindenwood?"

A wry smile fills his face. "You are an even cleverer girl than you were the last time we met. In fact, I was just about to impart this information to you. My scouts tracked the large group back to the main road toward Adelina. The smaller contingent continued north, not via the road, but through the woods on a straight course toward Lindenwood. I expect a report back from my men by the end of today."

It would be the perfect place to bring someone you wanted to keep out of sight. The area around the partially burned castle is nearly deserted. Most of the citizens who remain reside in nomadic villages surrounding the quarries. Across a large channel lies the Mainland—an easy route for someone who needs to disappear from Stewartsland all together. What if Liam has already been whisked away even further from our reach?

I add this to the list of worries which constantly plague my brain, an eternal commentary of dread. Is Liam injured? Is he hungry? Is he being mistreated? Around and around, the fears spin in my head like a giant whirlpool, which threaten to drown me if I don't stay vigilant.

"So, we need to get to the bottom of this matter for both Prince Liam's and your father's sake," Athos states.

A wave of relief floods me. Puck and I will not have to face this alone. I reach my hand across the table and the bandit takes it. "Thank you, Athos."

"You are most welcome. Now, let us figure out our next move."

The night turns cooler once the sun sets. Claude oversees the roasting of a decent sized boar; its scent suffuses the area and my stomach grumbles. When it is ready, the cook makes sure everyone gets their fair share. Athos, Puck and I sit back in the tent around the same table, plates full of steaming meat in front of us, when a tall man strides over to us.

"Luke!" I exclaim and jump up to hug him.

"Hello, Olivia,"

There is no trace of surprise in his voice to find me here. It is one of the things I love most about these men; they treat me as one of their own. He pulls out the fourth chair and joins us. The last time I saw him was in the spring when he came to the palace in search of a remedy for Athos' leg wound. Then, he had looked drawn with worry, but now he smiles, no such cares weighing him down.

"So, what news do you bring, my friend?" his leader asks.

"Strange activities up north," Luke begins, while Claude shuffles in to set a full plate in front of him. "The soldiers who arrived a few weeks ago remain encamped near the channel."

The cook eyes all of our dishes to make sure they are properly filled, then heads back to his station by the spit.

"There has been some activity in the castle, too. After a small party turned up last week, they have posted additional soldiers. They must hold a prisoner there."

"Liam," I gasp.

"The prince?" Luke questions.

"Yes," Athos answers. "It seems he was with the party who killed his guard."

"But I thought fire destroyed the castle," Puck says.

"About half of it still stands. Certainly some rudimentary rooms remain, if not more," Luke explains.

"They won't keep him there for long," I speculate.

"No," Athos agrees. "They will either move him—or kill him. We must act quickly."

"One other thing," the returning outlaw says, "a woman arrived two days ago. She entered on her own volition, so I don't think she is a captive."

"A woman?" I interject. All last fall and winter, when the king's life was under threat, there had been clues of an unnamed woman who supplied help to Lord Otto. This must be the person in question. "What did she look like?"

"She wore a hood, so I can't say."

All four of us sit in quiet contemplation, each digesting the new information. Liam's days are numbered, my father's days are numbered too. They both wait for someone to rescue them from their fate. The sheer weight of it on my shoulders is almost too much to bear. But if I don't help them, who will?

"We have to go. We have to get up there," I demand.

"Agreed, we leave at first light," says Athos. "Luke, get four men together to join us. We will go to Moosehead Canyon, leave the horses and travel the rest of the way on foot. Make sure there are men there to take the horses back here."

Luke nods, rises and, with a consoling pat on my shoulder, leaves the tent.

"All right, you two, eat up and get some rest. We don't know what sort of danger we are walking into. Now, if you will excuse me, I have some other matters to attend to."

Once alone, Puck ravenously shovels the meat down his throat, while I pick at my plate. All my cares have quashed my appetite. Having known me for all our lives, my friend leaves me be. Eventually, he saunters out and leaves me alone with my thoughts—a precarious place to be. They press against my mind like intruders trying to push through a door. If I allow it to open even a crack, fear will paralyze me.

Focus and assess. I repeat my father's favorite training phrase like a mantra. But to no avail.

I meander out from under the canvas canopy. The sun has all but set, only a last glow of orange tinges the western sky. Over and over, I replay the last conversation I had with Liam, so ordinary, so unemotional, so devoid of all I would have said if for even a moment I had thought it was our last. If Prince Stephan sends him to the Mainland, where would we even start our search? Or what if his cousin deems Liam too much of a liability? Will the threat of damnation continue to stay his hand? And without Liam, my father is doomed.

Suddenly, it all becomes too overwhelming. I sink down onto a log and stare blankly ahead. Fear, anger, and sadness each compete for attention. Crickets chirp their nightly serenade. A cool breeze lifts my hair ever so slightly. But I am numb to it all. Puck appears and sits down next to me.

"One of the men just showed me the most magnificent horse. Apparently, he was from far south on the Mainland. He was easily five hands taller than any horse I've ever seen." I am silent so he continues, "When we get back to court, I plan to speak to the Master-of-Horse about how we can get one."

"You realize we are both fugitives now?" The bitterness in my voice surprises me.

"Yes, well there is that," Puck chuckles. He hesitates, then adds, "I am sure we will find Liam and uncover exactly what is going on. Then everything can go back to normal."

"Normal. Sure. Except Liam will then be heir to the throne and I am not a suitable match." Even among all my troubled thoughts, this one has been like a pebble in my shoe, small in comparison, but ever irritating. "If we save Liam and my father exonerated, I still will not have what I want."

"Let's concentrate on finding Liam for now," Puck says. "That is enough to worry about."

"All right," I concede and lean my head on his shoulder.

He wraps his arm around me. We sit like this for a long while before finally heading to bed.

Liam

For the second full day, he rides bound to the horse with two men in front and two behind. Their course is due north. They must head for the coast where they can easily dispatch him to the Mainland.

His captors gave him a small meal this morning. Empty as it was, his stomach revolted against it, but in the end, he managed to keep it down. He will need his strength at some point. The side of his face aches where someone landed a good punch yesterday and his ribs are sore from the kick. Minutes drag on in the heavy heat while he attempts to remain alert.

A scout had arrived shortly before they left. The news must have assured the men they were not being followed. Though the pace is brisk, their mood is much more relaxed and so are their tongues.

"Will we reach Lindenwood tonight?" one man asks the leader.

Lindenwood? The name surprises him, yet the abandoned area and would make an adequate temporary hideout.

"Yes. Even though Jag said all is clear, Prince Stephan said to take no chances with time. Someone will come looking sooner or later."

They slow while crossing a particularly overgrown part of the road, a testament to the lack of travel in the area. He hopes to gain additional information, but his keepers say no more. Once the undergrowth lightens, they resume their speed. His head throbs in time with the horses' footfalls.

Many hours pass. In the murky twilight, the hull of the castle rises in front of them. Once through the gate, its damage comes into view. One side is completely collapsed. The other stands eerily whole next to the rubble. Men wait for them and hands roughly remove from his saddle. Two guards grab him under the arms and lead him away.

These new men navigate the still standing part of the castle as though they know it well. While many rooms suffered heavy damaged by smoke and falling debris, some remain inharmoniously untouched, blooming flowers in a barren field.

Into one such chamber, they shove him. A small oil lamp glows over an ornate desk. Bookshelves line the walls. Among the volumes, stand gloves, mini-carvings and other such trinkets. Maps lie spread open on a table, piles of papers litter the desk. It was once the office of someone important, perhaps King John himself.

With the table dragged out of the way, the rug underneath tossed aside. A trap door in the floor groans open, filling the room with a dank mustiness. All that he can see is the chunk of darkness is the top of a ladder. One guard climbs down.

"In you go, prince," the other orders.

He descends to the dirt floor. The first man busily lights two torches, which he sets in sconces on the bare wall. A leg manacle affixes to the wall like a menacing metal snake. The second man, who followed him down, shoves it around his ankle. It clicks into place. Without a look back, the guard climbs back up the ladder. The other comes over and pulls off the gag around his mouth. Dried blood flutters down around him.

"You will pay for this," he rasps, surprised how ragged his voice sounds. "My father will send his army to save me."

"Not likely, boy. At the moment, he thinks you are dead. At the hands of his Master-of-Arms no less. Don't hold your breath waiting for rescue," the captor sneers. He pauses at the bottom of the ladder and adds, "So you know, you can scream all you want down here. Nobody will hear you."

The guard climbs out of the subterranean chamber, pulling the ladder up after him. A small loaf of bread is tossed down in his wake before the door slams shut.

In the dim light, he surveys his surroundings. A cistern of water sits on the floor to his left, other than that the room is empty. He reaches for the bread, the manacle just stretching far enough. After a few bites and some water, he sits against the dirt wall. On his right, there is a doorway out of the room. It leads to the escape tunnel his father and Olivia used last fall. If he can somehow free himself from his shackles, he can follow their example. The chains, however, are new and strong. He does not have the wherewithal at the moment to counter them.

The thought of his father tears at his heart. Losing one son was devastating enough. To think he lost the other must be unbearable and, at the hands of his most trusted comrade, Jack Davenport. How could anyone believe it? Furthermore, why keep him alive and not kill him outright? He tries to puzzle it out, but no explanations make sense.

Olivia. His attention turns to her. She would never doubt her father's innocence. She will know Prince Stephan is the traitor. As his exhausted body drifts into an uneasy sleep, he thinks of her face and prays for her help.

"Rise and shine," a voice says, and my shoulder receives a rough shake. "Time to get going."

I sit up in my bed roll to see Puck next to me, the same bleary-eyed expression which must grace my face. Satisfied we are awake, the man walks off. We rouse from our slumber underneath a large pine. Needles carpet the ground, infusing the air with their woodsy scent. My friend rubs his eyes while I rise to pack up my few things. A spasm seizes my lower back the moment I stand. When I straighten up, every muscle in my body protests, not only from sleeping on the ground, but from the horse ride and the hiking from yesterday. The aches and pains remind me of when I first started training. In the few months I have been at the palace, I have allowed myself to become soft. Apparently, sparring here and there was not enough to keep me in shape.

It is not quite dawn. The sky lightens in the east, a sliver of gray against the inky dark. Claude happily brews porridge in the main encampment. Puck and I spoon it down quickly. The cook scrutinizes our every mouthful until the bowls are empty, then moves on to the next diners.

In a clearing a short distance away, eight horses stand at the ready. Despite the early hour, their tails swoosh in anticipation of the journey. I toss my belongings in the saddle bag on a brown stallion. His umber mane bounces silkily against his chestnut frame. He whinnies and shifts, eager to be off.

Luke comes to my side. "At least the weather looks to be fair today."

"Yes, that will help."

Athos appears out of the tree line and approaches. He has the faintest trace of a limp, which I had not fully noticed yesterday.

"It bothers him the most in the mornings," Luke states as though reading my mind. "Thanks to you, however, he is still here and in one piece. It was touch and go for a time after the infection."

"I'm glad I could help him. After all, what would we all do without him?"

"Indeed."

"Plotting without me, you two?" Athos teases when he reaches us.

We all smile genuinely, but the expression fades quickly from our leader's face.

"I have word of movement out of Adelina. They have noticed you are gone," he informs me. "A squad of men is on their way to find you. We must go in all haste."

The bandits have a network of scouts and checkpoints. News passes among them quickly. It is no surprise he knows of our pursuers. We mount and ride in single file with Luke at the lead, Puck and I in the middle and Athos bringing up the rear. The other men are not familiar to me, but if they have earned the trust of Athos, then they have mine.

Dawn brightens, traces of sunlight tinting the eastern side of the trees. Our path is overgrown but easily discernible. The horses have no trouble picking their way through the high grass. Although somewhat cool last night, the air quickly warms. Beads of perspiration form at the nape of my neck. We ride mostly in silence, a chorus of birds and insects our only accompaniment.

By mid-morning, my back aches. I curse myself for it. Last fall, when I snuck on the mission, I experienced no such pains. I will not allow my strength to soften like this again. Once we return, or rather, *if* we return, I need to make an effort to regain this strength. My body should be able to handle such activity.

We see no one on our journey. Athos knows the paths which are least likely to be watched. Our eight men and eight horses pass through the land unobserved. Shortly after noon, we arrive at Moosehead Canyon, a large hollow carved by nature into the side of some steep hills on our left. A vagrant tree clings to the slopes here and there, but mostly the terrain is rocky with overgrown brambles oozing out from the cracks in the earth.

As requested, men wait to take our horses. They herd them into a rudimentary paddock where a fresh pile of hay awaits. Athos and Luke speak quietly with another man, nodding at intervals. The rest of us mill around the area, some resting on boulders to enjoy a long drink of water.

"How is your back?" Puck asks, noticing me rubbing the stiff spot where hip meets spine.

"Sore. I let myself get too soft," I complain.

"I haven't ridden this much in a long time either. My backside is killing me." He rubs his bottom for extra effect.

"Great. And now, we get to walk the rest of the way," I joke, shouldering my gear.

Athos finished his conversation and motions all of us over.

"We will need to go through the forest to reach Lindenwood. The paths are all guarded. Percy, you will be our front scout. Our people will be at the usual rendezvous points, but there may be enemies in between. Bryan, you will cover our rear to make sure no one surprises us."

The two men nod, then head off in opposite directions. Again, I am amazed at the network of bandits Athos reigns over. If Prince Stephan is behind all of this, he likely forgot to take this important fact into consideration.

"There may be some tricky terrain. Hope you are up for the challenge," Athos says, strapping a quiver to his back.

Puck and I nod, but my legs are less than thrilled with the idea. My friend and I share a dubious look.

After a quick bite, the six of us remaining are off. The forest is dense, a plethora of bushes, trees, and overgrowth. Our progress is slow. Though we see no one, Athos and his men communicate with bird calls, the same ones which once saved King William and me.

The sun arcs across the sky, its rays dappling the woodland floor with pops of yellow light. A heavy, close air hangs around us and it is not long before sweat beads on my forehead. Finally, as dusk falls, Athos gestures for us to halt. He holds up a finger for us to stay put, then slips ahead.

Puck opens his waterskin and takes a long gulp, while two others wipe their brows with a cloth. I try to stretch out my legs, which became numb some ways back. The forest quiets in the gathering dark, the birds returning to their nests. Soon, the creatures of the night will stir, but for now, there is the peaceful silence of twilight.

Athos emerges from the trees. "All right, we make camp. No fires though. And we must be ready to move at a moment's notice."

He leads us through the trees to the edge of a large rise. A small hollow cut into the side has enough overgrowth hanging down to make our secret camp. Space is tight and with no firelight there won't be much we can do but sleep once the sun sets.

"Olivia," Athos calls in a whisper, "come with me. I want to show you something."

In the fading light, I follow the bandit up the rise. Huffing behind him, I use my hands at a particularly steep area to keep moving forward. As we ascend, I hear a faint roaring sound. It grows louder as we go, but I cannot identify it. When we reach the summit, Athos motions for me to stay low and we creep across the narrow flat top to look over the other side.

Now the tang of salt hits my nose in a crisp breeze. The roar I hear must be the sea, but there is another hum which layers over it. We crawl on our bellies to the far edge and Athos points down. Water breaks against the shore, the eternal thundering of wave on sand. Yet, the sand is not the only thing which greets the tide. The beach is full of gray masses broken up by flickering points of orange. It takes a moment to realize it is groups of men, their collective voices creating the hum, interspersed with campfires.

Not just men, but an army. An army of hundreds. An army which does not belong to King William.

"Who are they?" I ask in disbelief. "Where did they come from?"

"Largely mercenaries, I would guess, though some seem to have arrived from southern Stewartsland," Athos states.

A half circle of sun sits on the horizon, slowly sinking into the water's edge. Its fading light silhouettes the large force of men milling about the beach.

"Prince Stephan," I conclude, "it has to be."

They wait here for orders. He must intend to march against King William. But armies move slowly on their way. They would pass outposts and small settlements along the way. Surely someone would notice and send word to the king.

"He could not possibly advance this army to Adelina without the city being warned well in advance."

"True," Athos agrees. "He must plan to gain control of any scouts along the way and perhaps buy off the sentries who man the city walls. He has already begun turning people to his cause. With your father locked up and King William distracted, he must feel this army can reach the city."

"And if they breach the city walls with no warning, they will gain the upper hand in any ensuing battle. Then, he can usurp the throne." I muse.

The ocean extinguishes the setting sun.

"Come, we should return to camp," the outlaw instructs.

We slink across the open land on the summit. Descending the hill is a far more laborious task in the dark. Several times I almost lose my footing. On one occasion, Athos has to grab my shirt before I plummet out of reach.

Back at the camp, Puck spreads out our bedrolls under the cover of a large bramble bush which grows awkwardly out of the hillside. Thankfully, its thorns cannot reach us. We sit in silence and eat some beef jerky and an apple. There is no Claude to oversee a more substantial dinner. Quietly, I fill him in on what I just saw. Our meal complete, we recline next to each other. The others are hushed in the darkness, only a muffled voice or soft shuffling to be heard, lest someone detects our presence.

Through the gaps in the branches above me, the stars twinkle, blanketing the sky like fairy dust. Unbidden thoughts of Liam creep into my mind. Can he see the sky where he is? Certainly, my father cannot. The constant ache in my heart throbs full force in the night.

"Remember before training when we used to have make-believe night patrols?" Puck whispers. "We thought we were so grown up."

"Yes," I murmur, the smallest hint of a smile forming at the nostalgia. It has been years since my friend and I were allowed to have a pretend patrol. We would set up our camp at the far end of our property and imagine we were guarding everyone from the bad guys.

"We had some mighty adventures—in our minds at least," Puck jokes. "Of course, you were much tougher than I was. You still are."

"And you used to tell me stories about the stars." A pang of loneliness for those lost tales stabs me. "Tell me one now."

Puck is silent for a while and I wonder if he will speak at all. Finally, he begins in a voice barely above a whisper, "I just remembered one of my favorites."

"Once upon a time, an aging king and queen wished for a son to rule when they were gone. Unfortunately, despite their pleas to the Fairy Queen, they had a princess, their only child. In their eyes, the fate of the kingdom now must lie with her future husband, as a princess lacks the ability to rule. Yet, unlike other princesses, she did not sit around waiting to be saved and could often be found knee-deep in trouble. Her dismayed parents found this behavior unseemly in a princess and kept her locked away out of sight. There she would wait until a prince came to save her, then he would rule the kingdom, and all would be as it should be . Not resigned to her fate, she made a wish every day for the Fairy Queen's help.

"One day, a terrible dragon came down from the mountains wreaking havoc on the kingdom. It set fires with its breath and smashed buildings with its strong tail. Landing on the castle steps, it bellowed a mighty roar. The inhabitants, including the king and queen, all ran to hide.

"Alone and unguarded, the princess crept from her room, down the stairs and across the main hall to the entry. The dragon sat outside, smoke billowing from its snout. There was no indestructible mail or magic sword to help her when she faced the beast on the palace stairs. She was armed only with courage. Castle dwellers and townsfolk alike peeked from their hiding places to see the small girl stand against the raging monster.

"'Away with you,' she told him. 'You are not wanted here.'

"'Do you not fear me, girl?' it snarled.

"'Yes,' she replied, her legs trembling beneath her, 'but courage is doing the right thing despite being afraid.'

"At that moment, there was a flash of light and the dragon transformed into the Fairy Queen. 'You are brave and wise beyond your years. You will rule this kingdom well.'

"The people rejoiced, and the king and queen realized the princess was the ruler the kingdom needed. From this day on, they called her the Dragon Vanquisher. Peace and happiness reigned in the kingdom forever after."

Puck had indeed invented this very story in our youth. Then, it had contained a few more embellishments, including a pivotal role for the princess's best friend. But, all in all, it was the same story from all those years ago. He had spent an entire summer calling me the Dragon Vanquisher. At the time, it made me feel powerful, invincible, as though I could conquer any foe.

Now, all this time later, it leaves me feeling empty and powerless. Life has taught me fairy tale endings are harder to come by than people would have you believe. Tears form in my eyes and silently slide down my face.

My friend cannot hear or see me crying, but he has known me for so long, he instinctively knows. He rolls closer to me and gently strokes my arm until I finally drift off.

Athos rouses us early. When I stand, every muscle in my body protests. Again, I curse my lack of strength.

Although, why would I need my battle skills to help Niobe bring remedies to the village? A long sigh escapes my lips as my lost life of training dissolves in front of my eyes.

Breakfast is fast and unceremonious. Packs are hoisted, and we split into two groups of five. Luke disappears with one faction whose mission is to clear the way of any unwanted company. Athos, Puck, Percy, Bryan, and I head off a few minutes later.

Our track leads through the heart of the forest, where thick undergrowth obstructs our every step. Still, Athos knows exactly how to guide us, able to make the minutest adjustment in course to keep propelling us forward. What I judge to be about an hour passes before we halt. In unison, we reach for our water-skins. The canopy of trees holds the smothering air in place. My soggy hair clings meekly to my forehead. After a long swig of warm water, I wipe my brow on my sleeve.

"We are near the city walls," Athos announces.

City is a generous word for Lindenwood. It is merely a petite castle, smaller than some noble's estates, surrounded by a small marketplace and a handful of houses which make up a village. Since the palace stands partially burned and King John is dead, there should be little activity in the area.

We follow Athos to the edge of the woods. Before the break in cover, he holds up his hand and the four of us stop. Our leader steps to the edge of the tree line where his clear whistle rings out a singsong pattern. A second later, the same call sounds back in our direction. Stealthily, we emerge into an overgrown field, which runs to the city walls. Luke waits for us in the shadow of some bushes.

Once across, he nods and leads us along the edge of the barrier to a place where there is heavy damage. Between two collapsed sections is enough room for a person to maneuver through. One at a time, we squeeze inside the walls. We make for an alley which runs behind some shops. The passage was a busy place when the kingdom still functioned with shopkeepers and deliverymen alike haunting its confines. Now it is deserted of people with only a few forgotten objects; a shoe, a small axe, and the like littering the ground.

Luke halts and points for us to enter the back of one of the lifeless shops. Athos eases the door open and slips in with Puck and me right behind him. The others stay outside, taking up posts on either side.

The place is unnaturally quiet; the musty air almost a perceptible cloud. Bolts of fabric lie on tables and against the walls. A few have fallen to the ground haphazardly. Ribbons hang from rolls near the ceiling, long strands like the arms of sea creatures I have only heard tell of. At the front of the shop, a chunk of sunlight filters through the grimy window, a thousand specks of dust flittering in the rays.

I creep over to the frame of the window and rub a small section with my sleeve. Through the somewhat smudged pane, I can make out the side of the castle. A large portion of it burned and caved in the night we rescued King William. In a seam between where walls fell, there is an opening roughly the size of a wide hallway. Here the skeletal remains of a room sit, an undisturbed table and chair and a back wall complete with an intact doorway and several pictures. If one could block out the piles of rubble on either side where the walls used to stand, it would look like any ordinary room.

One lone figure mills about the wreckage, pacing a bit before settling on a large boulder flung down on the far side of the floor. Though he does not appear to be particularly worried about intruders, he is armed to the teeth. A sword hangs from his hip, a dagger from his belt, and a quiver and bow rest on his back. While we watch, he produces yet another knife from his pocket and scrapes at his fingernails with it.

"A guard?" I whisper.

"Presumably," Athos replies. "Let's wait a bit to find out exactly what it is he guards."

Puck finds two stools and brings them to the edge of the window. When he sets them down, dust clouds float in the muted light. Perched on one, I can see through the small circle I made on the glass. Athos stands in the shadow of the front door with a good sight line to the area in question.

Minutes drag along like wheel ruts in a long country lane, fading behind us into nothingness. Sweat runs down my brow, my back and my arms. There is no point in wiping it away. The flow is endless. The guard outside ambles around the half-standing room. At one point, he picks up a soot covered wooden chair. After an attempt to clean it off, he sets it upright and takes a seat right alongside the exposed interior door. For a long while, we all sit. Between the beastly heat and sheer boredom, I almost nod off.

Suddenly, the inner door opens, and a uniformed man comes out. The guard jumps to his feet as though stung while the soldier addresses him. I lean as close as I dare to the rub out area in the window to examine the new entrant. Athos, likewise, moves closer to the door. This man looks familiar, and I am certain he is one of Prince Stephan's men, who left with Liam on the trip north.

Puck comes to my side, and we watch intently. Two more figures emerge from the doorway—another soldier and a woman. All four converse with heads huddled close.

A startled gasp escapes my throat. Though I see her clearly, I still do not believe my eyes, yet they do not deceive me. Standing with the men is none other than Emily Crawford.

The conversation among the guard, the soldiers, and Emily is brief. Soon, one man strides down the rubble pile and disappears out of sight. Emily and the other soldier return inside while the guard resumes his seat.

"Was that Emily Crawford?" Puck's whisper breaks the silence.

"It was," I confirm, more than a hint of disbelief in my voice. Sinking to the floor, I try to collect my thoughts. Dust billows into the air around me like a cloud.

"Interesting," Athos murmurs, kneeling down beside me. Puck joins him and more grime puffs up, obscuring their faces for a second in the dim light.

"Well, it certainly explains a few things," I offer after a moment's reflection.

"Such as?" the bandit queries.

"Well, we know there was a woman helping the conspirators inside the castle. Emily must be the mysterious 'she' we could never identify. There was also an ominous comment she made when her sister, Jocelyn, left the palace about how Liam and I never knew what the future held. I wonder how long Emily has been Prince Stephan's ally."

"They have known each other their whole lives," Puck pipes in. "Maybe she always was."

In my mind, I see her and Prince Stephan returning from their picnic only days after Harold's death. Was she ever intending to marry Harold? It certainly seemed so. Yet she was clearly involved in the cousin's scheming before his untimely passing. Despondently, I absently draw circles in the dirt on the floor.

As though reading my thoughts, my friend adds, "At least there is no cloud of suspicion over the death of the late prince. That was most certainly an accident."

"True. And, however deep her involvement runs, we still have to concentrate on finding Liam. He must be inside somewhere if there are multiple soldiers stationed here."

"Agreed," Athos says, rising. "Let's see if Luke has found out anything useful."

We make our way to the back of the building and emerge into the alley. Percy stands alone in the shadow of a doorway up ahead.

"Luke and Bryan are still scouting the area," he informs us when we reach his side.

Though it is still warm in the alley, it is positively revitalizing compared to the musty shop. I droop against the wall like a wilted flower and take a long swing from my waterskin, the tepid liquid inside doing little to quench my thirst. The look on Puck's face conveys the same dissatisfaction.

A short time passes before we hear the approach of quiet footsteps. I rise, my hand taking hold of my knife, until Luke's soft whistle puts me at ease. Once Athos whistles back, the two scouts come into view. With only a series of hand signals, they agree to head out of the city.

When finally, in the cover of the woods, we huddle to discuss what each group has discovered. After Athos imparts our information, Luke tells us he observed lone guards posted at intervals around the part of the castle left standing.

"They must hold the prince inside somewhere," he muses, "but it would be impossible to gain entry without drawing attention to ourselves. Any sign of a skirmish and they can send backups from the beach as reinforcements. We could never get in and out before we were too heavily outnumbered."

In the silence which follows, I consider our dilemma. If we cannot gain access by traditional means, we must gain it by stealth. But how? Perhaps there is a secret entrance. Suddenly, I know the answer. When I look up, Athos smiles at me and I know he has the same thought.

"Let's head back to camp," he whispers. "Olivia and I have a plan."

"So how long do you think it will take to get to the exit of the escape tunnel?" Puck asks. He furls his bedroll into the kind of tight, even cylinder, which always eludes me.

Upon our return to camp, Athos and I explained how the tunnel could be our best bet at securing entry to the castle unnoticed. When King William and I had fled the burning castle through it last fall, we had passed at least one other entry point. Hopefully, this one still has access to the main building. The entry point the king and I fell through collapsed during the fire.

"I'm not sure, but hopefully we can make it before dusk," I state, hoisting my pack onto my shoulders.

Athos gives last-minute instructions to the men remaining behind before the five of us start out. We need more supplies this time—sticks and rags, extra knives, a length of rope. There is also an extra bag with food and water for Liam. We divide the additional burdens among us, each person taking his fair share.

Once again, we delve into the woods where there is not much of a path to speak of. Distracting thoughts of Liam hound my brain. Will we be able to find him? Will he be unharmed? How can we outrun the enemy back to Adelina? My fretting dominates my attention until I stumble on a downed branch and fall face first onto the ground. Puck helps me scramble to my feet. I force the worries away; otherwise, I will be of little use in this rescue. *Focus and assess.*

Last year, King William and I had followed the escape tunnel under the castle, eventually arriving at a dead end. The escaping Lord Otto had blocked the exit door with a pile of stones. Athos and his men had removed the barrier and saved us. At the time, my surprise kept me from truly taking notice of the area. I could never find my way back to the secluded spot where we surfaced. Thankfully, Athos can.

Our progress is slow, the forest so dense, the afternoon sun's rays barely reach through the leaves. Every once in a while, a shaft of light shines unblocked all the way to the ground, a flash of beauty in this hidden world.

Though I do not remember the exact location of the exit point, Athos' path seems purposely roundabout to avoid detection. A faint tinkle of water grows to a louder, voluble rush. Soon the sound is loud enough to show we are near the source. It is the Crystal River. Athos had led the king and me over a footbridge on our way back to camp. The water beneath it was far quieter than what I hear now. He must lead us to another crossing, though I see nothing but dense trees and boulders all around us.

At length, we clamber up a steep rise lined with overgrown vines, which snake down the side like an unruly head of hair. When I reach the top, I gasp. In the treetops which lean precariously on the banks of the water, a rope bridge runs across the river fully hidden in the vines. Trimmed foliage keeps any overgrowth onto the pathway across, but left to grow long enough to cover the end of the bridge from view when on the forest floor. Yet another of Athos' unending surprises.

Though it is a short trip across, it is rather wobbly. The water roars below but is barely visible through the vines. On the parallel shore, tress slant toward their sisters on the far bank. Anyone on the river would only discern the uppermost branches from each riverside, seeming to be joined a disorderly configuration of overgrown vines.

We step off of the bridge among the tops of some giant rocks. A path cut between two of them shields our descent back to the ground. The woods are less dense here so we must increase our vigilance. Although we encounter no one, we proceed with caution and our progress slows. Thanks to the season, we still have some hours of sunlight left.

When we finally reach the clearing where the trap door is located, Athos motions for us to stop. "You all keep watch from the cover of the trees while I look around," he orders.

Puck and I crouch between the trunk of a large Linden tree and some brambles. Percy and Bryan flank one on each side. A large hawk soars overhead, swooping in and out of through the treetops. It circles down and lands across the clearing on the bow of a dead, leafless tree. There it folds its mighty wings and watches us.

While we wait, Puck munches on a piece of jerky. He holds one out for me, but I shake my head. I am too edgy to eat. In the heavy silence, my heartbeats almost feel audible. After about thirty minutes, Athos steps out just underneath our new friend and motions for us. We rise as one to join him. The bird, unimpressed by us, takes flight, a shrill screech marking his departure.

"By all signs, there hasn't been anyone in this area for some time. Percy and Bryan, you two will stay here and stand guard until we return," the bandit instructs, then with a smile at me he adds, "Are you ready to go rescue your prince?"

The wooden door groans when pulled open, the hinges tight and tinged with rust. Since the abandonment of the castle by the former King John's staff, there must be no one who still sees to the upkeep of such things. A gaping black hole yawns before us, a dark rectangle in the falling dusk.

"Light two torches," Athos orders.

Puck pulls out two long sticks from the side of his pack while I grab some rags and string. After securing my items around the end of the stick, I pour a thick coating of oil on the fabric. Athos uses flint and tinder to light a small branch and uses it to ignite the torch head. A long, bright flame shoots into the air. When I finish wrapping the second stick, it, too, is lit.

The hole is illuminated, showing the ladder, which King William and I used to escape, lying flat on the dirt floor. Bryan retrieves a length of rope from his pack. He and Percy secure one end around a large boulder and return to us with the other.

"You two stay here and guard the entrance," Athos instructs the two. "The three of us will proceed."

The bandit takes the rope and ties it securely around his waist. He takes a torch from Puck in one hand. Bryan and Percy hold the slack of cord in theirs. Deft as a cat, he swings over the side of the opening and his men lower him down to the bottom, where he lands with the softest thud. Percy pulls up the empty line, which he holds out to me.

Handing my torch to Puck, I loop the rope around my waist, then take it back. Without nearly as much grace as Athos, I push off from the edge and the men lower me slowly to the ground. Dust billows around my feet when they touch down. The cable is returned. A moment later, Puck appears on his descent. When he unties himself, the two outlaws pull up the line. With a last nod at their leader, they shut the door tight.

"Give him your torch," Athos tells me, "I will lead with you next and him at the rear."

I pass my kindled branch to Puck. In the circles of light provided, I scan the room. The ladder has not only fallen, several rungs have cracked where they landed. A musty smell engulfs the space which even the burning oil does not fully cover. Our cursory exam shows no recent footprints in the chamber. Overall, the space is smaller than I remember; time having enhanced the memory in my mind's eye.

"No sign anyone's been this way in a while," Athos states. "still, we must stay alert, especially as we near the castle."

He guides us, sword drawn, with silent steps. I tiptoe behind, followed by Puck. An occasional pop from one of the torches is the only sound. Each time I jump when it happens. Our path incrementally slopes downward, where cooler air resides. It evens out, running on for a long time between its confined walls. When I walked through this tunnel with the king last fall, it had seemed endless and we headed away from danger, not toward it. Now, my heartbeat increases with every step.

Our leader slows and holds out his torch. For a short expanse ahead, the walls change from earth to stacked stone, mossy and cool to the touch. Wooden beams run across the ceiling. Tiny beads of water, which bleed through from outside fleck the stone and wood.

"This is where we pass under the river," I whisper back to Puck.

We continue on until the narrow hallway suddenly opens into a small circular chamber. Next to us, two other tunnels converge as well. The gate, which almost trapped King William, blocks the opening of one. This time, we do not need to guess which tunnel is the correct one, while three ways come together on this side of the room, only one continues on the other side. Our progress is slow, Athos ever vigilant for sounds or evidence of footprints. Gradually, the path slopes upward, before leveling out in a wider and much warmer corridor. Ahead the torchlight glints off sconces interspersed along the wall. They mark exit points into the tunnel from the castle. At the first one, a mere narrow opening cut into the wall, Athos halts.

"Wait here," he commands before disappearing inside.

In the dark, humid hallway, Puck and I wait. The passageway runs on for some length in front of us. I wonder how far along it the door where King William and I exited from is located. There will be no entry to the castle from that chamber. It had collapsed during the fire.

The bandit reappears. "There has been no activity in this place. We could gain access to the castle from here, but I would like to go a little further down the tunnel and gauge the use of other exit points."

My friend and I nod in agreement, falling back in line behind him. We explore two more chambers without incident. Then, as we creep farther along, the faint clink of metal rings out up ahead where a dim light filters out into the tunnel. Instantly, Athos motions us back to the last empty room.

"We will leave the torches in the sconces outside this room, in case we need them for a quick getaway," he whispers. "Ready your weapons and follow me."

The lights deposited in place, Puck and I draw our knives. Swords would be too large and cumbersome in such a small area. Pressed against the wall, we approach the lighted chamber. At the edge of the door, Athos holds up his hand for us to stop. My heart beats so hard, I cannot believe it is not audible to all. Ever so slowly, the bandit peers around the opening. He jerks his head back, an unreadable expression in his eyes. Taking my hand, he pulls me ahead of him and motions for me to stay quiet, an unnecessary reminder, I think, until I peek into the chamber.

A lone figure sits propped up against the dirt wall. His head droops over on his shoulder. One leg is shackled to an iron stake in the ground. Though the room is dimly lit, and the man is filthy almost beyond recognition, my heart still knows.

Liam.

Liam

Down in his dungeon, it is hard to keep track of day and night. Someone comes to refill the water and bring him scraps of food. He believes it to be once daily. If this assumption is correct, he has been here for three days now. The manacle around his ankle proves too secure. It withstands all his attempts at freedom. Condemned to wait, each minute is an eternity of uncertainty. Dank air fills the chamber. At first, he had longed for a blanket, but now his body hardly seems to notice the chill.

The door above creaks open. Odd, since they already brought him food just a few hours ago. A ladder lowers down. To his surprise, a woman descends. When she turns to face him, he gasps. It is Emily Crawford.

"That's right. It's me. I wanted to see you down here myself," she taunts. "Enjoy watching you wallow in dirt after the way you treated my sister."

His mind reels, the pieces hesitant to fit together in his muddled brain. Stephan's involvement was surprise enough, but how did Emily factor in?

She sees the confusion on his face, a smug smile alighting on her lips. "You've not figured it out, have you? That's all right. I'd be happy to enlighten you."

"Stephan and I have been planning this for a long time. It started by getting me selected as Harold's fiancée. That gave us access to the castle...and information."

He still cannot fully comprehend what she is saying. All his mind can visualize is his brother on the ground, an ugly purple bruise on his head. Surely, that had been an accident. He witnessed it himself. All he manages to mutter is "Harold?"

"Yes, by becoming his betrothed, I gained a foothold into the kingdom from where I could feed information directly to Stephan. We plotted to gain the kingdom last fall by luring King

William here to Lindenwood. Stephan enlisted Otto to help. He planned to march up here to help Otto vanquish your father, your brother, and you. Until you and that girl went and messed everything up."

"Otto," he says, chunks of the story taking form.

"Yes, he was our ally, but soon became too much of a liability. He lacked the patience needed for such vision, so we eliminated him. But not Stephan and me. We knew this would take time and careful strategizing. You thwarted our plan the first time, but it works out better this way thanks to your brother. His untimely death was actually rather timely for us."

"Did you ever love him?" Of all the questions he has at the moment, this one is the most pressing.

"I thought him a good man," she muses, "who, unfortunately, happened to be in the way of what I wanted."

"Which was what?" he asks, hardly able to look at her.

"To be the Queen of Stewartsland. Stephan and I have big plans with King Robert on the Mainland. We will mortgage off land and labor for very great profit."

"Only to your profit," he counters. "The citizens will live like slaves. It is the reason my father has kept us sovereign in the first place."

"I suppose that is one way to look at it. You and your father lack all vision for what riches could be at your disposal."

"It is called having a conscience. And Harold had one too," he fires back. "What if he had not died? Would you have married him?"

"Yes, for the show of it. Stephan and I would have continued to plan. It would have required a lot more bloodshed. With Harold gone, the only person to eliminate was you. That leaves Stephan as the rightful heir"

His blood boils at the treachery. How could he have not seen it sooner? Surely, his father could not be so easily deceived. "Do you honestly think you can get away with this?"

"I honestly don't see how we can't. Everyone believed our story about Jack Davenport. Of course, the twenty men we bribed to confirm the story made it all the more convincing. Now Stephan has the king isolated, lightly drugging him in secret to keep him under our sway. No one can get to him. No one has even questioned Stephan's actions. In fact, the only person who protested was Olivia, who apparently has set off on some ill-conceived rescue attempt. But no matter, she will be quickly disposed of."

His hands ball into fists.

"I see that got your attention. Even if she is not intercepted, it is no matter. Tomorrow you are off to the Mainland…if you make it that far. You see, Stephan has religious reasons for sparing your life, ones I don't necessarily support." She strolls to the ladder and climbs up two rungs. "One never knows, the trip to the Mainland could be fraught with all sorts of danger. Goodbye, Liam."

She is gone, with the ladder pulled up and the door shut firmly behind her. Anger festers in him like an infected wound. The betrayal of all of his family is almost too much to bear. Now his father and Olivia are in danger while he sits here impotently.

The next day, bread is tossed down from above. Feverish, he barely takes a few bites. He should eat more to keep up his strength. If they transport him to the shore to be taken to the Mainland, it will be his only chance to escape. Unable to swim, once aboard a boat, he will be trapped. Though he should plot how to get away, his head droops down and he slumbers.

The blow of a boot to his side jerks him awake. He had not heard the trap door open.

"You there, wake up." A giant of a man looms over him. It must be time to move him. "Move along now. Stand up. You are off to the Mainland. At least those are my orders, but if you give me any trouble, well then, I doubt you'll make it that far. Understand?"

His captor bends to unlock his shackles. With the click of its release, people emerge from the tunnel. At first, he thinks they are here to escort him away, but then he sees her face.

Olivia.

At first, I freeze, in shock that we have found him so easily. Athos pulls my immobilized body away from the opening. Puck takes a quick look for himself, a look of surprise across his face when he pulls back.

"Someone must guard him in the room above," Athos says. "We must not alert them to our presence."

Even as he speaks, the groan of hinges fills the air. A chuck of light filters into the hallway as the overhead door opens. The thud of a ladder hitting the floor is followed by scuffling steps down it. Athos, Puck and I press against the wall of the passageway, our knives still drawn.

"You there," a rough voice barks, "wake up."

The thump of a boot on a body makes me cringe. If it hurt Liam, he makes no sound.

"Move along now. Stand up. You are off to the Mainland. At least those are my orders, but if you give me any trouble, well then, I doubt you'll make it that far. Understand?"

Athos motions to the room. He is ready to make his move. Metal jangles followed by the unmistakable click of the leg shackles opening. With a nod at us, the bandit springs through the door.

The man is large, taller than Athos by almost two heads, but he is taken unaware. Athos holds up his dagger menacingly. However, the enemy simply knocks it out of his hand. They scuffle and Puck and I run in to assist. All three of us attempt to subdue the giant, who puts up a mighty struggle, throwing two of us off at a time before we continue our attack. Liam, startled by the whole affair, comes to his senses. He reaches for something in the corner, a clay cistern for water, and smashes it down on our foe's head, knocking him unconscious. Athos then locks the shackles firmly around his legs.

I rush into Liam's arms. "Are you all right?"

"Yes," he replies, though his red-rimmed eyes and haggard face tell otherwise.

While I touch Liam's face, not convinced he is real, Athos climbs the ladder and pulls the trap door closed, his spry feet on the ground a second later.

"Puck, break that apart," he indicates the ladder, and my friend cracks the rungs.

"Olivia, come here," the bandit orders. I walk to him, Liam's hand firmly in mine. He takes the bottom of my tunic in his hands and rips off a long strip, which he uses to gag the lifeless man. "No time for catching up now. We need to put as much distance between us and this place as possible. They will probably discover his absence sooner than later."

Hurrying back into the tunnel, we retrieve our torches and set out at a run. Though the passageway gradually narrows, we can still maintain a good pace. The circular chamber whizzes past. No need for us to guess which tunnel leads to freedom. Our steps are slowed a bit in the segment which passes under the river, the contracted space harder to navigate. Just after this point, Athos motions us to halt. In the silence, we strain to hear any sounds of pursuit, but there is only silence. This does not deter the bandit, who sets out again at a breakneck speed.

Behind me, Liam labors to breathe. The exertion which normally would not faze him, sounds as though it becomes too much. Clearly, he was not a well-treated captive. By the end, even my lungs burn, each step a more valiant struggle.

Bursting into the exit chamber, the four of us double over on hands and knees. Athos regains his breath almost immediately. He whistles his special call, which is answered at once, and the door in the ceiling groans open. We shield our eyes against the brightness which floods in. Seconds later, a rope dangles down.

"You first, Your Highness," Athos says and helps Liam secure the cord around his waist.

While the men hoist him up, the bandit has us shatter the already broken ladder into even smaller pieces. The dry wood brittle with age snaps easily, leaving no remnant large enough to be useful for anyone who follows.

The line drops back into the chamber. I take it and tie it around me, then give a little tug. Steadily, the rope raises me up to the top, a hand waiting to pull me into the warm sun. Bryan's smiling face greets me, and he helps unbind me.

In the full daylight, I get my first good look at Liam. He is filthy from head to toe, his hair matted, and his face covered in a full beard. His clothing is ripped, the scraps which remain stiff with grime. A dirt and blood caked bandage wraps around one forearm. Though captive for just a little more than a week, he looks gaunt and pale. My heart breaks for him.

While they lifted Puck and Athos up, I embrace my prince. His arms envelop me, flooding me with a sense of relief and security. He may not look like my Liam, but our bond remains ever the same.

"I knew you would come," he whispers, the words a warm breath in my ear.

"Put boulders on the door," Athos orders his men. "That may buy us precious time. We will go to the tree village. I will send scouts at dusk to replace you. I expect a full report."

The men nod, already dropping heavy stones on the trapdoor.

"Come, you two," he says, prying us apart. "We aren't safe yet."

He plunges into the forest with the three of us on his tail.

We take a circuitous route, picking our way through the wilderness. Brambles tangle our feet below, while low-hanging branches swat at our heads. Athos finally stops in front of a rock the size of a small building. It stands in a dense area of woods, an odd sort of sentry amongst the tree trunks. A figure leaps down from its peak, causing all but our leader to jump.

"Any activity, James?" he whispers.

"None at all."

Athos nods, satisfied with the answer. "Now follow me," he says to us.

He guides us around to the other side of the rock and scales it. At first, he seems to glide up by some kind of magic, but when I look closer, small footholds are discernible. When he reaches the top, we watch in surprise as he pulls himself through the tree boughs. The leaves rustle and he disappears.

"Well, I guess that would be the way to the tree village," Puck murmurs.

"You go," Liam says to me. His voice sounds raspy and tired.

Tentatively, I grab a fingerhold and pull myself up. The climb is fairly easy, when you forget the fact it is about as tall as my house. At the top, I find my balance. Liam and Puck gaze up at me expectantly. They look smaller than I would have imagined, but I am too curious to let the height bother me. Above my head, a canopy of branches hangs, their leaves forming a thick, green blanket. Hands suddenly appear in front of my face. I hold up mine and they grab my wrists and pull me through the foliage where I am deposited on a solid piece of wood. Once firmly on my own feet, I look at my surroundings.

The platform forms a circle around a tree trunk. Off of it, on four sides, run rope bridges, much like the one we used to cross the river. These connect to similar platforms on other trees. As far as the eye can see, these passages span in all directions a hidden labyrinth over the forest. Certain platforms have ladders ascending higher up the trunks to some unknown destination.

"There you go, Your Highness," the hoister says.

Liam comes to my side. A moment later, Puck stands next to us, surveying the area in the same quiet amazement as we do.

"This way," Athos points. "Mind your steps. The bridges are sturdy, but too heavy a footfall sends debris down to the forest floor. Best not to alert anyone to our presence, as I am sure they will be looking."

The unfamiliar overpass is wobbly under our feet, but each successive step becomes steadier. Athos leads, with me behind, followed by Liam, Puck and two members of the outlaw band. Our steps are light and methodical. Around each pathway, trimmed branches allow enough room to pass, but the rest are left full of leaves for coverage. On our way to the palace, I would never have suspected this existed right above my head. We come to another platform encircled tree and head off to the left. At this point, I only have a limited idea of what direction we head in.

There is little talk among us other than whispered directions from the front. Each time, I convey them to Liam. He smiles reassuringly, his white teeth a bright contrast against his filthy skin. Though not cool, the air is refreshing, the natural shade keeping the sun's rays at bay. Every so often, at a break in the leaves, sunlight dapples onto the bridge like large shimmering drops of water. Warmth huddles in these scattered patches, a reminder of the hot summer beyond these trees.

On one platform, we stop for a drink. I share my skin with Liam, who greedily gulps down most of its contents. With an apologetic shrug, he hands it back to me.

"Don't worry," Athos says, "there will be plenty of water soon."

With no further explanation, he continues across another bridge. The secret world of Athos never ceases to amaze me. The never-ending excitement and adventure. All those months in the palace had deadened the part of me which craved this. It faded so far into the background, I hardly remembered what it felt like. These past few days have me feeling more alive, more myself, than the previous six months put together. Yes, my love with Liam is wonderful, but I lost a piece of myself which I am thrilled to reconnect with.

A stray thought tugs at the corners of my mind, always there, even when dwarfed by other worries. If I cannot have Liam, what then? Perhaps this could be a life I choose instead. Hopefully, Athos would let me join him. I glance longingly back at Liam, whose eyes narrow in puzzlement at my expression. Could I ever leave him? The choice does not seem mine to make.

The trees ahead are more densely packed together. Crossing a final bridge, we pass through a leaf barrier and the tree village lays before us. Dozens of crude shelters hover on platforms amid the closely knit trunks. Hammocks stretch among the branches under tarp-like coverings. A large rectangular floor between two mighty oaks holds a bench and various sized crates for storage.

Athos alights on this wide space and motions for us to sit. A man, who melts out of the shadows, speaks with him softly. The three of us plop down heavily on the wooden bench. After some discussion with him and the two men who accompanied us, our leader excuses himself and they all cross a bridge and disappear somewhere in the village.

Liam's brow drips with sweat, his hair dangling limply on his shoulders. He leans back to rest his head on the tree behind the bench and shuts his eyes. Instinctively, I reach out to feel his forehead.

"What's your diagnosis?" he asks, not moving.

"Slightly feverish, Hold on." I rummage through my pack until my hand hits upon the desired vial. "Here, drink this."

He takes it from me and tips his head back, emptying the contents in one sip. Meanwhile, I check his pulse and do as much of a general assessment as possible. "Did they feed you?"

"Barely."

Gently, I pinch the skin on the back of his hand and note how long it takes to return to place, a rudimentary test for dehydration.

"You need to drink as much water as you can," I order.

"Yes ma'am," he jokes, but softens when he sees my concern. "Don't worry. I will."

The man to whom Athos spoke returns with a tray of cheese, dried meat, fruit and a large pitcher of water. He sets it down on a barrel nearby. Puck and I dig right in, but Liam only sips some water.

"You should try to get something in your stomach," I tell him when he makes no attempt at the food. I break off a small hunk of cheese and hand it to him.

"She's very bossy," he says to Puck.

"Always was," my friend agrees with a wink at me.

"Just eat you two," I snap.

"See? Told you." Liam smiles.

I only shake my head. He nibbles on the cheese, which is enough for me. Leaning against his side, he wraps an arm around my shoulder. There is so much to talk about from the kidnapping, to how to make it safely back to Adelina, to what the future holds. But for this moment, I settle back and enjoy the simple comfort of his embrace.

"And so, in the end, it was Athos who found us," I explain to Liam in between bites of an apple. Puck sits next to us, stuffing hunks of cheese into his mouth. We have been alternating parts of the story to bring the prince up to date.

"Then, Athos and Livy thought of the escape tunnel," Puck says, food still in his mouth.

"I am surprised they had you down there. It was so easy for us to get you," I ponder.

"They obviously did not count on Athos aiding you. It was clever of you to think of him," Liam praises. "Would you have been able to find the trapdoor in the woods without him?"

"Not as quickly, if at all," I admit, twirling the empty core around aimlessly in my hand. "It would have taken days of searching."

"They were planning to move me to a ship headed to the Mainland." He takes a miniscule bite of bread, his appetite not fully returned.

"Honestly, I'm surprised they did not already. It's still a wonder he didn't kill you outright." I shiver at the thought.

"Stephan fears that. He doesn't want royal blood on his hands for fear of eternal retribution. Emily, however, pushed for it. She saw me as the liability that I was. Eventually, I think she would have convinced him to silence me forever."

"I'd like to say I can't believe she is involved, but the more I think about, the more I can," I sigh. Liam had always had misgivings about Emily, though I think neither of us would have imagined the depth of her treachery.

Before we can speak any further, Athos rejoins us. Pulling up a barrel, he sits down in front of us, a pensive expression in his eyes. We wait to hear what news he has found out.

"Clearly, we must get His Highness back to Adelina. Needless to say, all ways will be watched by our enemy, who must know by now of his escape. I would like to wait until morning to move. I want to see where they deploy the most men before I plan our route."

"Surely, the main road will be heavily patrolled," Liam speculates, "which eliminates our fastest path."

"Not necessarily the fastest," Athos replies cryptically.

"Then what is?" Puck and Liam question in unison.

"The river," I blurt out, the answer coming to me like a bolt of lightning.

"Exactly," Athos agrees. He smiles at me with the same look of pride Father does when I figure out something in training.

"But we would be sitting ducks on the water, exposed on all sides," Puck points out.

"Yes," Athos concedes, "there will be eyes on the river, which is why we will need to blend in."

"How?" asks the prince.

"As ordinary people—bargemen, traders, fisherman, anything which does not draw suspicion. Additionally, men will shadow us along the shore and try to pick off any small band the enemy may station along the way."

"I suppose it is as good a plan as any," Liam says, tossing his last crumb of bread to a nearby bird, which greedily swoops to grab it before flitting back into the trees.

"I must go make preparations. You three will be safe here. I will have some hot food brought in a bit, then get some rest. We will depart early."

When he rises, Liam stands as well and puts his hand on the outlaw's shoulder. "Thank you, Athos, not only I, but my kingdom will forever be in your debt."

The bandit nods in gracious acknowledgement. "Your father and Olivia's father are honorable men. Neither deserves this hand dealt to them. I could not live with myself if I did not see this right."

Once Athos is gone, a young man appears and directs us to a secondary platform suspended between two widely gaping branches higher in the tree. Several hammocks swing from makeshift posts. A tree stump serves as a rudimentary table. He brings us a large cistern of warm water, which we use to wash our hands and faces. Liam wipes his face dry on a cloth, a hint of his handsomeness peeking through the scruff.

Puck lays his pack down and climbs into the nearest hammock, folding his hands behind his head. Liam jumps into the next one. He motions me to join him. I hop in next to him, then lay my head on his chest. His heart beats steadily against my ear, a comforting sound. The slight fever seems to have broken, which also reassures me.

"I still can't believe my father believes your father betrayed him," he exclaims.

"I don't think he wants to believe him, but what is he to do in the face of twenty men's testimony?"

"I don't know. I just wish he had put up more of a fight," he replies sullenly.

"He is still grieving for Harold," I remind him softly.

"My question," Puck says, "is what was Emily Crawford hoping to gain out of throwing in her lot with Prince Stephan? She was set to marry Harold and ascend to the throne with him"

"Yes," I agree, "Why help Stephan last year when she was secure in her position?"

"Because that was their plan from the beginning. While they held me captive, Emily taunted me about my brother being but a mere pawn in their game."

My heart hurts at these words. Prince Harold was a decent man, who would have made a noble and fair-minded king someday. He deserved far better in life than the likes of Emily Crawford.

"For years," Liam continues, "the idea was in his head to usurp the throne. Though he would have rule fairly independently in the south once his long ill father passed. In some twisted way, he felt entitled to it. Knowing he would need a powerful ally in Adelina, he was instrumental in Emily's selection as a match for Harold. Somewhere along the way, he found Otto and began planning the conspiracy. When Arthur lay dying last year and all duties fell to Stephan, he finally saw his chance."

"So, they promised Otto Lindenwood and Emily was to rule by Stephan's side?" Puck queries.

"He had Otto set the trap in Lindenwood. My cousin intended to march up with his men not to aid my father, but to ambush us from behind. The bulk of his men were in the dark as to the actual plan, which worked out well for him when he arrived, and my brother had matters in control. He simply pretended to be there to help. Now that I recall, Prince Stephan had seemed oddly dazed the day he arrived in Lindenwood last fall. He did not share the same delight as everyone when King William returned unharmed. I had written it off to general shock and surprise at the situation.

"Otto escaped that day, of course, and fled down to Prescott where Stephan hid him with the clueless Brother Alastair. Stephan tried to work with Otto and form some kind of plan, but my father's half-brother was too obsessed with his own idea of revenge and took matters into his own hands. And we all know how that turned out."

"So, after Harold's death," I say, "he came up with the plan to get rid of you, thereby making himself the rightful heir to the throne."

"Exactly." Liam heaves a tired sigh. "I guess he didn't count on you messing up his plans both times, Olivia."

"Actually, he didn't count on Athos the first time, and he made that same mistake again this time," I counter.

The young man reappears with some hot food and warns us to be quiet. Enemy men search the woods below and come ever closer. He vanishes as quickly as he came, leaving us a bit unnerved. We sit in silence, straining to hear any movement on the forest floor, but the humid summer air swallows up the careful footsteps of our pursuers, never reaching our ears. After a while, we all drift to sleep safely in our hidden sanctuary.

Athos rouses us early the next morning. Darkness still clings to the leaves in the treetops. Once again, we follow him across a labyrinth of bridges high above the forest floor. His steps never falter even in the dim light, yet his slight limp is always visible. The growing roar of water fills the air as we near the Crystal River.

"Here is where we go down." Our leader stops abruptly, causing Puck to walk into my back.

Rudimentary rungs hammered into the side of a tree lead the way down. We leave the platform and descend to the earth. The air is immediately fresher, as when one opens the window in a stuffy room. Ahead of us, the trees thin out, more sparsely spaced down to the waterline. Sunlight glints radiantly off the river in patches of iridescent shimmers. Two men wait at the bottom of the ladder, a large chest on the ground between them.

"All right then," Athos says, "time for disguises."

An assortment of garments fills the chest. He holds each one of them up for inspection before distributing them to us. In the end, Athos and Liam dress as bargemen for the vessel they will pole. Puck, joined by Luke, will be fishermen who will shadow the barge in a skiff. Lastly, I am handed the clothes of a peasant boy.

"Since you are accustomed to dressing this way," Athos teases, while the men whisk the chest back to whatever hiding place it came from.

A wide flat scow waits at the river's edge. Several crates and trunks supposedly filled with merchandise take up much of the space. The fishing boat sits nearby, several rods and creels in its hull. The water laps gently at the shore.

"Ever poled one of these, Your Highness?" Athos inquires.

"Can't say that I have," Liam counters affably.

"Once we get into the middle of the river, the current should pick us up and make easy work of it."

He deftly leaps on board and holds out a hand for me. From a large stone, I make the jump onto the barge. Liam hops on behind me and the craft pitches from side to side.

"Careful not to fall in now, my prince, I don't have time for a heroic rescue," Athos says with a wink.

Liam's face fills with trepidation. He does not know how to swim, a fact we discovered on our last mission. I place a consoling hand on his arm, and he smiles at me.

Athos pushes off from the shore, sure-handedly maneuvering us to the water's center. Liam helps him to steer it until we head straight downriver. I climb on top of a crate to keep out of their way. Back on shore, Puck and Luke climb into the small boat. The fishing poles stand upright while they use small oars to navigate their way behind us.

"Go in that trunk, Olivia," Athos orders.

Inside, I find three bows and quivers full of arrows. I hand them each a set and strap the last one around my shoulders. Out of curiosity, I peek into a couple more crates. There is some food and empty water-skins in one, some daggers and snares in another. None are filled to capacity. They are more for show.

"Olivia, if they fire at us, Liam and I will fire back. You must toss the cargo into the river, so we move faster."

I nod at him, a knot forming in the pit of my stomach. We are wide open targets out here on these boats. It would be all too easy to pick us off from the cover of the riverbank. The fishing boat keeps back a few hundred yards. Puck's head bobs slightly from side to side, the brim of his large hat flopping slightly in the breeze. Hopefully, they have some bows and arrows to defend themselves as well. Somewhere on the tree lined shore, Athos' men watch over us, stationed at different intervals along the route. Yet despite this, I still feel like a giant bulls-eye in the center of the river.

The sun rises bright and full across a clear blue sky. White clouds float past, like giant dollops of whipped cream. Morning turns to afternoon, the merciless heat battling against the cool spray of the water. There has been little talk among us, our focus on the banks on either side, scanning for any movement. A swift current moves us at a faster pace than I would have imagined, far speedier than any journey by road.

I nibble on some dried beef, handing a hunk to Liam. He takes it absently, his mind elsewhere, but at least he eats it. His color returns slowly and there has been no more trace of fever. Hopefully, all the ill–effects of his captivity will disappear.

A shrill whistle cuts across the air, startling us both. Athos merely whistles back. "So far, all clear," he informs us.

The mid-day sun arcs across the sky toward the west, but still many hours from setting. Once it becomes dark, we will have to go ashore. Though we have made good time, we will not make it all the way to Adelina before then, unless Athos has another trick up his sleeve.

Before I can even ask, the *swoosh* of an incoming arrow rings across the river. Instinctively, we duck. The projectile does not have the strength to reach us and crashes into the water a few feet shy. Athos and Liam draw their bows. When the next shot flies out of the trees, they fire back in that direction. A few more arrows target us, one piercing the side of the trunk I crouch behind. Following instructions, I push off two large crates, which bob in our wake, and the barge speeds up a bit. Our foes hold the advantage of us being in full sight, while they enjoy the benefit of cover; extra speed is one of our only advantages at the moment.

Behind us, Puck and Luke fire at the shore, their tiny boat rocking precariously with each shot. The clang of metal on metal erupts from the banks. It fades off behind us. Ahead, a man emerges from the trees, hands waving. Liam aims, but Athos pushes his weapon down. "That is my man. We must go ashore here."

They take up the poles and guide the barge to the riverbank. Just a few feet from shore, Athos jumps in and orders us to follow. We grab our backpacks and leap in behind him. Our scow, with its contents, spins off downriver. Two men rush from the forest to pull us ashore. They share a hurried whisper with their leader.

"Follow me and draw your swords," Athos orders.

He leads us into the thick of the woods, where we crouch through the dense undergrowth. Additional men appear and fan out around us, including Puck and Luke, wet and winded from their adventure arriving ashore. Our movements are quick and quiet, every ounce of attention focused on the surrounding forest. Athos stops and holds up his hand. We all freeze. Ahead of us, on the edge of a path, stand four soldiers. A series of hand gestures sends certain men to strategic spots while the rest of us wait.

"We need to eliminate them and flush out anyone else in the area," he whispers. "Do not let any of them escape."

At a signal, one of the bandits leaps across the space. He shoves a knife deep into the back of one soldier, who slumps to the ground. His comrades yell out and draw their weapons. Two more outlaws hurtle out of the woods to engage them. From farther down the road, shouts ring out along with the pounding of footsteps. Four more enemies appear, followed by more bandits. Athos motions to us to join the fray. A fierce battle ensues.

All around me are the clashes and grunts of combat. Liam crosses swords with a man nearby. Though he is not large, Liam's reflexes are slower than normal. I jump in to assist. For a moment, the attacker hesitates, perhaps confused by my stature. The prince uses the opportunity to strike the side of his head with the hilt of his sword, knocking him out cold.

Behind us, Puck fights with a behemoth of a man. My friend struggles to hold his own against a crushing barrage of blows. Liam and I spring to his aid. It takes the might of all three of us to slow our adversary. His giant arms, the size of most men's thighs, bulge with exertion. Blood gushes from a gash in his forehead down his side of his face. When it reaches his mouth, he merely spits it in our direction.

With a swoop of his arm, our foe hammers Liam against a tree, where he crumples. There is no time to check on him. Puck and I assault him with strikes which he easily parries. No matter what angles we take, he is unstoppable. In the confusion, however, he does not notice Liam rising. A moment later, a sword runs him through from behind. He staggers a few steps and slumps on the ground.

Immediately, the three of us whirl around, our weapons at the ready for the next enemy. But only Athos' men remain standing, though one grasps his shoulder where blood escapes in a dark red flow. While others tend to their wounded comrade, Athos and Luke motion for us to follow them and we are off. In the ever-darkening woods, we trudge over brambles and logs, each step a treacherous undertaking. Our senses ever heightened for any sound which would indicate trouble.

Just when I am convinced Athos is lost, he stops at a large rock. A heavy curtain of overgrowth flows down its side, like a green waterfall. Around it, downed trunks pile haphazardly across the landscape, all covered in dense brush and vines, menacing silhouettes in the dusky light. Our leader blows a soft whistle, which the rock itself seems to answer, until the leaves are pushed aside, revealing a door-like opening. We slink inside of a dimly lit cave.

"Here we will wait out the night,' he informs us, "and get you home tomorrow safe and sound, Your Highness."

And once again, Athos saves us.

"It will be hard to get anywhere near the palace. The city will be closely watched," Liam speculates.

We sit alone in a small nook in the cave wall. Dim firelight glows around us. A few yards away, Puck gathers with Luke and other outlaws describing the battle in the forest. My friend's eyes dance in excitement while he shares some particular detail.

"Puck seems to be enjoying himself," Liam vocalizes my thoughts.

"Yes," I agree. "Life with Athos is never boring. In fact…"

"In fact, what?" he asks when I pause.

"Well, it's just that once we get you home safely, your father will not let us marry." Again, I halt, but his eyes plead with me to continue. "And, I thought, rather than hang around and watch you marry someone else or get shipped down to Prescott, that maybe…"

"Go on," he says in barely a whisper.

"Maybe I would see if Athos has a place for me." I say.

Liam sighs, "Olivia, there is no way I will not marry you. You risked your life to save mine. Do you really think I will let anything come between us?"

"But…"

"No buts. If my father will not allow us to marry, we will leave. We can both join Athos' band as far as I'm concerned."

It is an idealistic thought, not a practical one. We both know it. "The kingdom can't have its crown prince running around with outlaws. You are obligated to serve…"

He cuts me off. "Not without you."

There is no point in arguing with his stubbornness. If we get him home safely, the reality of the situation will sink in soon enough. With Prince Harold dead and Prince Stephan a traitor, there is no one but Liam to inherit the throne. Any abdication of his duty would result in a struggle for the reign of Stewartsland from both ambitious people within the kingdom and power-hungry leaders without. In this cave, still in danger and removed from the expectations of his father, Liam can easily think we are fated to end up together. I am not so sure, silently vowing to join Athos if I cannot have my prince. For now, though, I must enjoy what time we have.

"I'm sure Athos would be thrilled to have us," I tease, in an attempt to lighten the mood.

"Indeed, he would. And we would never be bored," Liam chuckles, squeezing his arms around me. I settle against him and try to banish the future from my mind.

We set off early the next morning, before dawn is even a full-fledged thought. A gray brightening gives shape to the surrounding forest. After some deliberation last night, our plan is to gain access to the palace from a remote area. The wide expanse leading to the main gate of the city provides no cover, and according to scouts, is under close observation. I explained how the back gate, where Niobe and I gathered holly, was situated. This seems our best option.

Our trip is not a long one. We covered more ground yesterday than I thought. The woods soon thin out from the chaotic tumble of trunks near the cave. A small pond comes into sight, one Lydia and I have fished at many a time. More familiar sights between my family's house and the palace pass by. Half of me wants to turn and run home, but it would provide neither me nor my companions any safety.

In all, we total eighteen men, though most remain out of sight, scouting all sides of the path ahead. Athos sent additional men to tactical positions into the city itself. At length, Athos, Liam, Puck, Luke, and I arrive at the holly grove. The thick branches provide nice cover for the five of us. Crouched amongst the prickly leaves, we survey the back gate.

"You are certain only one rusty bolt holds that door shut?" Luke questions in a whisper.

"Yes. At least, the last I saw it." Perhaps our enemy has discovered its weakness and fortified it.

"Even if no one stands guard nearby, which is almost unthinkable, breaking it down will garner attention," Athos muses. Certainly, shattering of the door would alert half the village to our arrival.

"We could try to scale it," I suggest, though with what I do not know.

After a moment's thought, our leader answers, "It is risky. It would leave us exposed on both sides of the wall for longer than I would like. Any other ideas?"

Moments pass as each of us ponders a solution. A scraping noise brings us back to reality. It is the gate's rusty bolt, which groans when pulled out of place. Slowly, the door opens. Our hands fly to our weapons, but we remain huddled in the bushes, watching. The world stands still.

A figure emerges. Not the soldier we were expecting, but a young man. I recognize the shock of black hair and the farrier's apron. "It's Franklin."

"You know him?" Athos asks.

"Yes."

"You trust him?"

"Yes."

Franklin does not seem to have a purpose for exiting the gate. He mills about near the open door, anxiously scanning the woods in front of him.

"Luke, cover Olivia while she calls him."

I rise, the bulk of Luke looming behind me and step from the shadow of the bushes. "Franklin," I rasp somewhere between a whisper and a strangulated shout.

He startles a little before spotting me. Slowly, he approaches, and I creep out a few feet to meet him. Luke moves with me as though we are physically connected. When the young man stops in front of me, I whisper, "We need to get inside the gate. Is it guarded?"

"I can't believe she was right," he mutters in disbelief.

"Who?" I ask, but suspect the answer even before his reply.

"Niobe. She just sent me to open the gate for you. I thought she'd gone mad."

The hairs on the back of my neck stand up. The healer's sixth sense never ceases to astound me. Athos, Puck, and Liam slip out of the bushes to join us.

"Do any guards stand inside, son?" Athos asks.

"No, sir, not near this gate"

"Then we must move quickly.'

We file into the ten feet of open space between the holly grove and the gate. Instantaneously, soldiers melt out of the tree line, their weapons drawn. Stephan knew we would try this point of entry. The men close in on us on all sides.

"Run," Athos orders.

We sprint to the gate. A mere foot away, an enemy barrels up on our right. Puck and I round to fight him. More attack on the other side, with Luke and Liam ready to counter. Franklin stands in the gateway uncertain what to do. The four of us dispatch of our combatants only to see more spring from the woods. They outnumber us.

Athos, whose leg has slowed him down, stands between us and them. Each of us breaks toward him.

"No," he yells, swinging his blade at the first man to reach him. "Go. Get them past the gate. That's an order."

Luke falters for a split second but obeys. He grabs all of us and pushes us to the gate. Once certain we will make it, he runs back to his leader. Just as we cross through, numerous bandits spring from the trees and rush to the aid of their heavily outmatched leader. The last thing I see before Franklin slams the gate shut and draws the bolt into place is Athos falling to the ground.

Franklin leads us to the far left behind the latrines. The odor is oppressive in the summer heat, but they provide good cover. We encounter no soldiers; he must know where guards stand stationed throughout the city. Surely, they concentrate on the main gate and surrounding woods, confident they could cut us off. But all will be alerted to our presence now.

"Should we try to get to Niobe's?" I ask.

"No," Franklin replies, "she told me where to bring you."

We trudge across an unplanted back field, the grass up to our knees. A lone man works here, piling some rocks into a handcart. He looks at us questioningly, but continues with his task. The terrain turns rougher with brambles weaving across the stony ground where it runs up to the walls which ring the palace. There stands Niobe, a tiny form against the dark rock structure. I run to her.

"Welcome back, child," she says, enfolding me in her thin arms. The others come up behind me and she embraces Liam as well.

"Thank you, Franklin," I say. "We could not have gotten in without your help."

"Yes, well done, boy," Niobe agrees. "Now go home and pretend none of this ever happened."

He nods in acknowledgement before slinking back the way we came. I hope he makes it home without incident, but right now, there are bigger problems to address.

"We must get Liam to the king before Prince Stephan can stop us," I explain. "Then we will go to Helen," the healer determines.

"Yes, my mother will help," Liam agrees.

"Follow me and stay quiet," she orders, a lively spark in her eye I have not seen since her injury.

We press against the wall and proceed in single file. About two hundred feet later, she pauses by some overgrown bushes where she retrieves two shovels and a basket, along with several hats typically worn by servants who work in the sun. Liam, Puck and I look at her blankly.

"You boys, put on the hats and take the shovels." Quickly they comply.

"Are we going to try to dig under the wall?" I blurt in confusion; well aware we do not have this kind of time.

"Goodness no," she chuckles. "These are just tools a person would usually carry out here."

"Oh," I say, mollified, "that makes more sense. And me?"

"You will hold my arm while I carry the basket, a young boy helping an old woman," she answers, shoving the last hat on my head.

While the implements give a sense of purpose, the three of us are filthy, our clothes stained and tattered. Anyone who looks closely enough will notice something is off.

"Up ahead," the healer instructs, "there is a door to a stairway which leads up to the royal wing of the palace."

"The assignation door," Liam mumbles.

"The what?" Puck stammers.

"It allows people to come and go privately when they meet with the king or queen so as not to be seen by the general court," he explains.

"When I last checked," Niobe says, "there was a sole sentry there. We will need to overpower him to get inside. I am sure the top of the stairs is watched as well."

Liam and Puck rest the shovels on their shoulders, my friend even whistling a popular working tune for effect. Niobe and I fall into step behind them; she leans heavily on my arm to navigate the uneven terrain. Sure enough, a few hundred yards ahead, a lone guard comes into sight, standing outside a small door which leads into the palace. He spots us and watches attentively. We maintain our leisurely gait.

When we are about ten feet away, he huffs, 'Who are you? What are you doing here?"

He is young, perhaps fourteen, and his tone holds only feigned authority. Of course, it makes sense to put an inexperienced soldier in a post unlikely to see any action, a situation which works to our advantage.

"Good afternoon, just tending to some routine grounds keeping," Puck answers brightly. "Sure is a hot one, huh?"

The boy's brow narrows while he digests this information, but his posture relaxes. We stroll even closer while I marvel at my friend's convincing performance. Puck has taken to all the danger and intrigue more capably than I would have ever imagined. Liam, too recognizable, keeps his head down, lest he be recognized.

"It looks as though it has been messy work," the sentry comments, a look of distaste in his eyes as he surveys us.

"As a matter of fact, it has been," Puck agrees, taking a step to his side.

Quick as a flash, Liam pounces, spinning the boy around and placing a dagger at his throat. A frightened bleat escapes the surprised guard's mouth.

"No screaming now, understand?" the prince commands. His terrified captive nods meekly. "Do you have the key to this door?"

The boy shakes his head furiously.

"If you knock, will someone come down?"

"Y… y… yes,"

"How many people?"

"Just one I think."

"Do you know who I am?"

"No," he sputters.

Liam turns him around, the knife never leaving his throat. "I am the crown prince of this kingdom. Any move you make against me from this moment on will be considered treason."

The sentry's eyes widen. "Yes, Your Highness."

"Now, you will help me gain access to the castle."

"Yes, Your Highness," the boy's voice shakes, "I am sorry, Your Highness. I am Eli. I would never betray my kingdom. We were told you were dead. The citizens do not officially know this yet. We are to keep it quiet for now according to…"

"Prince Stephan?" I query.

"Yes," he confirms.

"My cousin attempts to usurp my throne," Liam says, and lowers the knife. Eli makes an awkward attempt to bow. Nervously, he looks over Puck, Niobe and me.

"If I knock loud enough, the guard upstairs will come down. He should be alone, but be wary. He is a loyal supporter of Prince Stephan. I take it he will not be happy to see you."

"No indeed," the prince confirms. "Olivia, Puck, draw your daggers and flank me."

When everyone is in position, Liam nods to the boy, who bangs on the door. For a moment, there is silence, then the stomp of booted feet ring out, louder with each descending step.

"What's in your head, boy? This better be good," a gruff voice demands from the other side of the door.

When it flings open, a stout soldier appears. He barely has time to react before three daggers point at his throat. With baffled astonishment, he regards us until his eyes rest on Liam. His expression hardens.

"Alert..."

His scream cuts off with a sickening bonk. Niobe clocked him in the head with Puck's shovel. He falls unconscious on the ground. The rest of us stand frozen in disbelief.

"Quickly now," she orders, snapping us back to reality.

"Eli, run to the citadel," Liam orders. "Tell Sir Michael Queen Helen requests his presence immediately. Speak to no one of me. Do you understand?"

"Yes, Your Highness. It will be done." He rushes off as though death itself chases him.

Meanwhile, Puck and I drag the soldier into the doorway where his insensible form takes up most of the landing. I help Niobe navigate over him and we mount the steps, ready to attack anyone who confronts us. At the top, another door stands open and we come out into a small vestibule off the side of a hallway. Liam peeks down it for a second before turning back to us.

"There are at least three guards at the end of the hall outside my mother's chambers. I am sure there are more by my father's. If we cause any kind of commotion, we will be quickly outnumbered."

"Not to worry," Niobe whispers. "Follow me."

On one side of the vestibule, a large tapestry hangs depicting maidens enjoying a picnic on the grass, while men admire a stag they have brought down in the background. The healer lifts a corner, ducks behind it and disappears. Niobe is well familiar with all the secret passageways in the castle.

I follow her, with Puck and Liam behind me. She waits inside, holding the secret door open until we are all safely inside. The entrance to the corridor shuts tight and we plunge into utter darkness.

"Now just give me a moment," Niobe's soft voice requests in the black which surrounds us.

After some rustling and clicking, a small lantern lights up. Cognizant of every detail, the healer has carried both the lamp and the supplies to light it in her basket this whole time.

Cobwebs choke the passageway on both the walls and the random objects which litter the floor. A candlestick, a glove, yellowed by time, and a folded piece of ancient parchment, a few of the items visible in our small circle of light. Puck leans against a beam and a mushroom of dust rises into the airs, the grime at least a half an inch thick on all surfaces.

"Here, child," the healer holds out her arm. "You help me keep my footing while I guide us."

As quietly as we can manage, we head off to the right. Luckily, the layer of dust coating the floor muffles our footsteps. A few turns later, I have lost all sense of direction, but Niobe is confident of our course. Liam and Puck follow so closely behind us, they walk into us when she suddenly stops and holds the light up to the wall. The faint outline of a door is visible.

She places a finger to her lips and presses an ear against the door. After a moment, she raps quietly on it, three fast ones followed by two slow. We stand stock still, the deafening silence enveloping us. Then, the same knock pattern sounds from the other side of the wall. Niobe repeats hers a second time. There is a click and the door slides open.

"Niobe, what are you doing here? You must be quiet. There are guards right outside my door," Queen Helen says in an urgent whisper.

"I have brought you something to cheer you up," Niobe answers. She nudges Liam into the room and we all step in behind him. It is the queen's private chambers.

Despite his dirty, disheveled appearance, she recognizes him at once. Mothers just know. A slight gasp escapes her lips before she flings her arms around him. They stand for some time in a silent embrace. When they part, she hugs both Puck and me, her eyes wet with tears.

"Thank you, Olivia," she whispers in my ear.

"Mother, you must take me to father. The sooner he learns what a traitorous scoundrel his nephew is, the better."

"I can't," she replies.

"Why on earth not?" I exclaim as loudly as I dare.

"Prince Stephan has many men here. He has undermined the soldier's loyal to the king with his accusations against Jack Davenport. With both Harold and you dead, Prince Stephan would be the rightful heir and your cousin wants his reign to start immediately. The king does not wish to see bloodshed, see innocent men killed for an outcome which seems inevitable."

"That is not the father I know," Liam protests. "He would not let his kingdom be stolen right out from under him."

"Grief affects people in ways we cannot imagine. When news first came of your death, the king plunged into despair. It is unnatural for a father to outlive both his sons. Now Stephan keeps him almost as a prisoner in his own chambers. The short times I am allowed to see him, he is not himself. He seems addled and confused. Niobe and I are certain he is being drugged, but cannot come up with a way to get alone with him."

"Yes, Emily said he was being drugged. I must get to him. We must cut through any fog. Together, we can take back the kingdom," Liam says.

Queen Helen has us settle down in chairs, even dragging two out of her bedroom. She orders her servant to bring us some water. The girl looks frightened by the turn of events and with her duties fulfilled, disappears into the bedroom. We quietly discuss different options for getting Liam to the king or vice versa in a palace full of soldiers whose sole mission is to prevent just that from ever happening. By now, Prince Stephan would know Liam had escaped Lindenwood. It is not hard to guess where he would have headed. A loud rap on the door makes us all jump.

"Hurry, into the bedroom," the queen orders. We pile into the chamber, where the scared young girl backs against the wall. "Sally, you must answer the door. It's all right, child. Just stay calm."

With the tentative movements of a newborn fawn, the girl teeters out of the room. Liam pushes the door until it is just ajar. We draw our weapons and some deep breaths and wait. The rapping grows louder before we hear the door click open. I strain to hear what they say.

"Your Highness, this man told us you had requested his presence," the soldier's voice is unfriendly, clearly someone hostile toward the queen.

"I am no mere man," Sir Michael's gruff voice states. "I am the King's Master-of-Arms."

"For now," the soldier sneers.

Liam and I exchange a panicked look. In all the confusion, we forgot to tell his mother this detail. There is no need to worry; however, Queen Helen is savvy enough to play along.

"Yes, Sir Michael, there are some matters regarding Jack Davenport's pending execution I would like to discuss with you."

I cringe at the sentence and Liam rubs my arm soothingly.

"Perhaps I could be of use in your discussion," the soldier offers.

"No, that will not be necessary. Maintain your post," the queen answers. "Now, if you will please excuse us."

The door closes solidly against his feeble protests. Sally scrambles back into the bedroom and plasters herself against the wall. I smile at her, in an effort to allay her fears, but it does little to soften the terrified expression on her face.

"Sir Michael, I need to show you something, but you must remain quiet," Queen Helen instructs. She pushes the bedroom door fully open. "Come out."

Liam steps into the main room with the rest of us behind him. The knight's eyes widen before filling with tears. In an uncharacteristic breach of protocol, he wraps the prince in a giant hug.

"You are a sight for sore eyes." They step apart. Sir Michael runs his hands through his shoulder-length gray hair and his expression hardens. "I knew Prince Stephan was untrue. How did you escape?"

"Olivia came to rescue me with…some friends." He omits any mention of Athos.

The knight turns his attention to where I stand just behind Liam. To my surprise, he enfolds me in an embrace.

"Thank you, Olivia. Your father will be overjoyed to know you are safe."

"My father is innocent. We can prove that now."

"Indeed," he agrees, then addresses the prince. "What do you command?"

"Go to the citadel. Release Sir Jack and gather all men still loyal to my father."

"There are many, but there are at least an equal number who are loyal to your cousin."

"Many of whom think I am dead. Let's see where allegiances lie once they see me alive and well. Go now and await my orders."

"Yes, Your Highness." He bows.

"Wait, I have an idea," the queen interjects. "Sir Michael, tell any non-loyal soldier who asks that you and I discussed Sir Davenport's execution and I instructed you to bring him before the king. Make it appear he is still a prisoner. Have the loyalists follow behind as though they want to witness the occasion. Can you be outside the king's chambers in a half-hours time?"

"Yes, Your Highness." He touches Liam's arm once more, almost as if to make sure he is real, before taking his leave.

"Mother, take us through the connecting rooms to father's chamber," Liam says.

The king's and queen's chambers are joined by two small ante chambers and a large reception room. I have studied layouts of the castle with my father when he went over different emergency scenarios. Theoretically, Queen Helen should be able to walk right through to the king's rooms whenever she felt the need.

"That is not a good idea," she replies. "Many in Prince Stephan's inner circle sit there all day. They spy on whatever interaction I, or anyone else for that matter, have with His Majesty. I have taken to just going to his main door, where they may or may not let me see him."

We all deflate a bit at this news. I thought getting into the castle would be the hard part, but with access to the king so heavily guarded, our options are limited. Liam furrows his brow. I am sure he debates his odds of simply rushing through the rooms to his father.

"Here is my plan," the queen states. "We will give Sir Michael his thirty minutes, then I will go to see my husband. That will not raise any alarms, as I try every day. Niobe will lead you through the secret passage to the hallway right outside His Majesty's chambers. Once the knights arrive, you will join me, and we will demand to see the king."

"What if they won't let us?" I voice the question on everyone's tongue.

"We will cause a loud enough commotion to draw not only the king's attention, but the notice of other palace residents. Witnesses would be to our advantage. In fact, Sally, come here."

The maid timidly steps from the bedroom where she has been listening the whole time. "Yes, Your Highness?"

"Sally, you can come and go from this chamber relatively unnoticed. Please find my secretary, Bartholomew. Give him this note." She hastily scrawls a few lines on a piece of paper and hands it to the girl. "Keep that hidden and tell no one of your mission. Tell them you go to fetch me a snack. I am relying on you. We all are."

The maid's demeanor changes, a look of determination filling her youthful face. She takes the folded note and hides it in her sleeve. With a nod from the queen, she strides out the door, where the guards, not seeing any threat in a young servant girl, pay her little mind.

"I instructed Bartholomew to find as many loyal courtiers and servants as he could and come to the king's chamber," she advises.

"Well done, Mother," Liam praises, kissing her cheek.

There is nothing to do now but wait.

Time drags slowly. Puck, Liam and I shift from foot to foot and alternately pace the bedroom floor where we hide. The queen stares out a window into the courtyard below, so deep in thought, her empty eyes see none of it. Niobe simply relaxes in an armchair, head back, eyes closed, as though this is merely any other afternoon. She has said little during our planning and I wonder what her intuition tells her about our chances.

At the appointed time, the queen retrieves us from the bedroom. The healer relights the lantern she had extinguished, takes her basket on her arm, and leads us back into the dark corridor.

"Wait for my signal," the queen reminds us against the shutting door.

The trip to the hallway outside the king's chambers is direct. We make only one turn before Niobe holds up her hand for us to stop. Through the wall, we can hear the muffled voices of two guards talking casually to each other. From the sound of it, they are close enough to touch. Hardly a breath passes among us as we wait. There is an abrupt clanking noise when they jump to their feet.

"Your Highness, does the king expect you?" one exclaims.

"Expect me? I'm his wife. I do not need to make an appointment. Please let him know I am here." Her regal composure impresses me.

The chamber door groans open and one must step inside to deliver the message. From the other direction, a clamor arises—the sound of many footsteps. They ring off the marble walls, growing louder as they approach.

"What is that?" stammers the other guard.

"More visitors perhaps?" the queen drawls.

When the men march into the hallway outside the king's chamber, dust shakes off the walls of the hidden doorway, wafting to the ground to settle again. We listen intently, awaiting our signal to exit.

"What is the meaning of this?" a voice booms. Chills run down my spine at the sound of Prince Stephan.

"I have some business to discuss with my husband regarding Sir Davenport," she affirms. My heart leaps, knowing Father is right outside.

"And what exactly is so important that you all had to trudge him up here?" Stephan asks, the edge in his voice apparent.

"I need him to arrest you for treason," she says calmly.

He gives a derisive snort. "On what grounds?"

Liam forcefully pushes open the secret door and steps from the tapestry which conceals it. Puck and I follow in his wake. In a t-shaped hallway, about twenty men stand with the queen. Along a side hall, Bartholomew arrives with a legion of courtiers. They freeze at the sight before them.

"On the grounds that I am very much alive," Liam avers.

An audible gasp escapes many lips, soldier and courtier alike.

Prince Stephan blanches for a split second before his eyes harden. "I have control of this army, plus an army marching on Adelina as we speak. Your rag-tag group cannot stop the inevitable. You're too late, cousin."

The men with the queen draw weapons and stand behind Liam. Puck and I join them. My father holds out his hand to me and pulls me to his side. Behind us, courtiers seem uncertain what to do, but are too enthralled to look away. Intrigue such as this is a rare spectacle in King William's court. If it came to it, I wonder how many would stand with Liam.

"Guards!" Prince Stephan calls.

Doors open all along the corridor with soldiers flowing out like ants from a disturbed nest. Three times as many men surround us. Our group turns back to back, holding weapons out against the enemies who encircle us. Queen Helen is safely at our center.

Stephan surveys the situation smugly. "Take all these *traitors*," he takes pride enunciating the word, "to the citadel."

"You dare call us traitors?" Liam shouts.

There is a scuffle as he tries to reach his cousin. The queen attempts to follow him but a soldier roughly pushes her back. I push him with equal force. All around, men strain against one another. At any moment, the scene could break into an all-out melee.

"Enough," Liam yells, wrenching his arm out of a man's grip. "You want my father's kingdom? My kingdom? Then fight me for it, man to man, not that I find you worthy of even this title."

"I don't have to fight you. I didn't even have to kill you to come in here and gain this kingdom for my own. You have already lost."

"Gain by treason and treachery," Liam accuses. "What have you promised these men for their allegiance?

How can they expect any loyalty back from you when you have shown you have none?"

The two now stand face to face, Liam a full head taller than his cousin. For the moment, all movement has ceased as everyone strains to hear their conversation.

Prince Stephan shakes his head in mock disappointment. "Cousin, have you not realized that loyalty is given to those with power? I hold the power in Stewartsland now. Anyone not loyal to me will be disposed of in one manner or another soon enough."

"I will be dead before I see my kingdom in the hands of the like of you," he snarls.

"That is the general idea," Stephan sneers.

Liam tries to get his cousin in a chokehold. Pushing and punching break out all around me. The mass surges toward the two princes. A sea of arms and torsos swallow me, bodies banging against me in every direction. Tripping on something, I look down to see one of Queen Helen's silk slippers, who is caught in the fracas somewhere. Straining to catch sight of her or Liam, I lose focus. My cheek smashes into a large man's back, a cry of pain lost in the cacophony. I try to brace myself on him. If I fall, I will surely be trampled.

Suddenly, someone booms, "What is the meaning of this? Stop this madness at once!"

Instantly, everyone freezes and turns toward the authoritative voice of King William.

Soldier's lower their weapons and the courtiers, who have not run for safety, all drop to a knee. Through multiple heads and shoulders, I see him, looking older and more ragged despite his courtly robes. Niobe stands just behind him. In the confusion, she snuck into his chamber. She gives me a cryptic smile and looks down at her hand, where she holds a small red vial, the spirits of ammonia. They are used to restore consciousness and mental alertness. Whatever sedatives Stephan used on the king are now counteracted. His eyes are now keen and alert.

"Nephew, what is going on?" he demands.

"I think I could better answer that," Liam says, stepping forward.

The monarch pales and holds onto the doorframe for support. "Liam," he whispers, "but how?"

"I think there has been a terrible misunderstanding," Prince Stephan says, perhaps hoping to explain away his treachery.

"There has been no misunderstanding," Liam avows. "You faked my murder and blamed Sir Davenport. Now, you have an army marching on the city ready to claim my father's throne."

King William, who has recovered from his initial shock, regards his nephew with a hard stare. "Is this true?"

Stephan is silent for a moment; forever calculating what words will help his position the most. He decides the truth is the best option. "Yes, uncle, it is. The overthrow of your kingdom is nearly complete. I think you will find more people loyal to me here than you expect.

"Nonsense," the king blusters. "Take him into custody."

My father and Sir Michael reach for the traitorous prince, but swords raise against them. I lift my sword and point it at a man who threatens Father. All around the hallway, men, some brothers in arms since boyhood, face off. Additional soldiers filter into the corridors drawn by the commotion. The newcomers, unsure of what they have walked into, look around confused. Courtiers still stand wide-eyed along the walls.

"I think you will find I am in charge here," Stephan asserts. More men close in around us.

Liam lowers his sword and pushes past his cousin. He climbs onto the pedestal of a pillar. All eyes follow him.

"Gentlemen, my soldiers, my brothers," he addresses the crowd, "my father has dedicated his life to this country. Through his valor and strength has Stewartsland been a safe and prosperous kingdom. Those of you who came to serve Prince Stephan value lies and greed above honor. Those of you who were born and bred here, who enjoyed the benefits of this good king's rule, yet turn against him now. I ask you why? Look into your hearts. You already know the course which is just."

Around me, men pause and look from one prince to the other. Some who oppose us I have known since childhood. Until now, they placed their loyalty in Prince Stephan as they assumed he operated under the king's authority. Now, comprehension lights in their eyes while Liam continues.

"Perhaps you threw in your lot with this traitor because you thought I was dead. You thought with no heir the kingdom would be vulnerable and my cousin seemed the safest option. I understand and you will not be held accountable for any actions prior to this moment. But, as you can see, I am very much alive. I love this kingdom and I love my father. I will defend them both until my last breath. Now I ask of you—will you do the same? Will you stand with me? With my father? With everything which we hold dear?"

His impassioned plea holds the room in suspended animation. All eyes lock onto him, some wet with tears. In him, I see the king he is meant to become. My heart swells with pride, yet also a bittersweet pain, for I know now, no matter how much I love him, I can never stand between him and his destined fate.

"Fine words," Prince Stephan sneers, "but words are no match for swords. Take him away!"

At first, no one moves. Slowly, one man repositions his sword from Sir Michael to point it at Stephan. "I stand with Prince Liam."

"Aye," another voice vows, followed by a chorus of affirmations all around the hallway until only a handful of the insurgent prince's loyalists remain. The turn of events surprises them.

"Sir Michael, take this man and his traitorous followers to the citadel," King William commands. "You are no nephew of mine."

This time, a clear majority steps up in the king's favor. The conspirators are herded together before a large contingent with Sir Michael at the helm escorts them away. Applause breaks out among the courtiers when they pass.

"You won't be clapping when my army arrives." Stephan yells back to them, "This is not over!"

An uneasy murmur filters through the crowd. We won this battle, but the fight is not over yet. Stewartsland remains in danger and King William's place is still far from assured. Silence descends with everyone's full attention directed at the monarch.

"The rest of my men, gather your fellow soldiers, any you can find in the city or nearby country. Amass in the main courtyard. My orders will follow shortly."

Once again, the hallway springs to life. Men take off in all directions, happy to have a sense of purpose in the shadow of an oncoming threat. Courtiers zip off to spread the word far and wide of the spectacle they just witnessed. As the area empties, Queen Helen goes to her husband and they share an embrace. Liam joins them and they immediately wrap him in their arms. "My son. My son," the king repeats softly.

Father finds me and hugs me tightly. He feels frailer than I remember. Puck waits for his turn behind me; my father holds a place in his heart as a surrogate parent. Niobe touches my arm, a wide smile on her face. None of this would have been possible without her and she hushes me when I tell her so.

"Indeed, Olivia is correct," King William affirms. "Once again, you rescue me from peril."

He kisses her forehead. Uncomfortable with the praise, the healer merely hands him more smelling salts with some instructions and excuses herself. We watch her tiny form shuffle down the corridor like a feather floating on the air.

"Father," Liam says, "we must prepare. A large host marches on us from the north."

"How many?"

"Several thousand from what Olivia saw. Isn't that right?" He motions me over.

"Yes, I would estimate two and a half thousand at least."

"We cannot muster many soldiers from outlying areas. A good five hundred or so will be the total of our forces," the king muses. "Will this be enough to make our stand?"

"It will have to be." Liam says.

"Perhaps the enemy will have second thoughts when they find Stephan is no longer in control here. They are a mercenary army, after all. It is payment they want more than any particular outcome."

"True," the monarch says. "You say you saw this army, Olivia?"

"Yes, on the shores of Lindenwood."

"Lindenwood?" he asks, puzzled.

"Yes," Liam replies, "That is where they held me prisoner."

"Why there?"

"Apparently, there were ties there. The diplomatic visit last fall was supposed to be a trap whereby Prince Stephan would get control of Stewartsland and Lord Otto of Lindenwood."

Liam fills his father and mine in on all the details he learned during his captivity, including Lady Emily's participation and Otto's deviation from the plan. King William's eyes smolder with anger by the time he is done.

"Olivia, how did you even find Liam, let alone free him?" the queen questions, her voice filled with wonder.

"I had help from Athos. Again."

"Indeed?" says the king. "Once again, I owe that man. If we ever cross paths, I shall have to reward him."

"He is here," I exclaim, visions of the bandit fighting outside the back gate fill my mind. "He helped us get Liam home."

"Well, by all means, fetch him so I can properly thank him."

Puck leaves with me. He has instructions to go to the stables and summon the Master-of-Horse to the king. We part at the bottom of a staircase and I hurry across the back fields to the gate. Several people gather just inside, their attention drawn to a spot on the ground. An uneasy flashback to the day of Harold's death flashes through my brain. I quicken my pace. Closing in on the area, I see a tiny figure with white hair hunched over something. My heart stops. Of all the familiar faces, I know who to ask.

"Luke, what happened?"

He turns to look at me as though confused to be addressed. His eyes are red with tears. "I couldn't get to him in time. There were too many of them. I tried to…" he trails off, his shoulders wracked with sobs.

On wooden legs, I pass through the crowd and kneel next to Niobe. Athos lies beneath us. His face is as white as snow, a thin sheen of sweat on his brow. The healer examines a large wound in his side. I do not need any expertise to know it is grave. While she works on him, I take his hand. His eyes open, glancing around before falling on my face. At first, the stare is blank, but then, a gleam of recognition.

"Miss Olivia," he barely manages.

"Don't talk," I order. "Save your strength. You will need it to recover."

Niobe and I lock eyes and I see in hers the same defeat which was there when Becky lost her baby. There would be no recovery. A lifetime of thoughts passes through my mind in this moment; a moment which at once lasts forever yet is over far too quickly. Feelings of anger, grief and unfairness, of helplessness and love, all stampede toward me in a surge so powerful, I can barely find the wherewithal to move.

"I am so sorry, Athos. This is my fault." I squeeze his hand harder, even as his grip weakens.

"No. Do not be sorry for this… you are a brave and clever girl… no, woman… knowing you will live your life to the fullest makes my death easy to face." He shudders, his breath coming in ragged spurts.

"I love you," I whisper.

"And I you. 'Tis a noble death…one can ask for no more. Be strong, my sweet Olivia. Things are as they should be."

His eyes flutter a few second and close. A long breath quivers out of his body. Then, he is still. Tears run freely down my face, dropping onto our still interlocked hands. Niobe strokes my hair but says nothing. Luke kneels next to me, his anguished cries echoing over the silent crowd.

Athos' body seems smaller in death; his commanding personality always lent it size. Still, I clasp his hand, unwilling to let it go and face life without him. A chasm of empty sorrow opens in my heart as Niobe pries my fingers free and pulls me to her breast.

Grieving is not a luxury time affords me, or any of us, at the moment. An army marches on the kingdom. King William, though saddened to hear of Athos' passing upon my return, must see to his people. He sends men to retrieve the bandit's body to lay it in the chapel and assure Athos' men more will be done when the situation allows.

Liam embraces me, though not before I glimpse myself in a mirrored section of wall. Tears have left a track of flesh-colored skin down my otherwise filthy face. My weary, swollen eyes are bloodshot. A few months ago, I would have been embarrassed to have Liam see me in such a state. Now, such trivial issues hardly matter.

He fills me in on what has transpired. "We have sent men to gather the closest townspeople and have them brought inside the city for their safety. Sir Michael deposited the prisoners in the citadel and now sees to the positioning of men along the upper walls."

We are in a large reception room on the main floor of the castle. It is a place where citizens may petition the king on certain days of the month, an orderly affair. Today, a more chaotic scene plays out. The king, my father, and some advisors pour over a map on a table, which now stands in the center of the room. Queen Helen stands to the side, listening intently. Soldiers dash in and out to collect and execute orders. Palace staff moves unnecessary benches to the side walls where they sit in a haphazard pile.

A senior knight rushes into the chamber. He has a brief but animated exchange with the leaders at the table before rushing back out again. The monarch motions Liam and me0 over. We approach the group, who all look grim at whatever prospects they have been discussing.

"Sir Jacob just informed me the bulk of the soldiers in the city remain loyal to me. Those few who were not have been dealt with accordingly. This will still leave us greatly outnumbered. I have sent a small detachment to Prescott, though it is unclear to me whose side the remaining soldiers in Prince Stephan's home city are on. Either way, they are days away from being able to assist us."

"We must rely on diplomacy then," Liam states. "Prince Stephan bought this army's allegiance. They hold no loyalty to him other than their pockets. We must somehow negotiate with them."

"Hopefully, when they see you are firmly in charge here and not Stephan, they will want to make a better deal for themselves," I add.

"Perhaps," King William sighs. He looks us both up and down. "You two should go clean up. There is time yet before any action will start."

"All right," Liam agrees, "A quick bath and changing out of these rags will make me feel better."

He takes my hand to leave, but notices the stricken look on my face.

"What?" he asks.

"It's just that…" I trail off while everyone looks at me expectantly. "It's just that I have no room here at the palace any more…so I'm not sure where to go or what I could put on."

Liam's eyes narrow. In all my descriptions of what had transpired in his absence, I omitted the detail of Anne's and my eviction from the grounds.

"What happened to her room here?" the prince snaps accusingly at his father.

Before the abashed monarch can reply, the queen jumps in. "Not to worry, Olivia. You will come to my chambers to wash up."

She takes both my elbow and her son's and guides us out of the room, hopeful Liam will drop the subject with his father. He does, though I see the anger smolder behind his eyes. When we are safely out of the room, she wraps an arm around him.

"I am so happy you are unharmed," she says.

"Yes," he answers, "it's a good thing *Olivia* came to save me."

The boiling anger evident in this response causes the queen to check them. "This is a conversation for another time."

Liam still fumes, but remains silent. He gives me a peck on the cheek at Queen Helen's doors before striding off to his own chamber. When we enter, poor Sally leaps to her feet, looking as panicked as when we last saw her. The queen reassures the girl how well she did, which seems to calm her somewhat. Then the monarch instructs the servant to draw me a bath. Happy to have a stress-free task to perform, she leaps into action.

My jerkin unbuckles easily. Several clumps of earth fall to the floor when I remove it. Sally must help me peel off the tunic, stuck to my skin with sweat and dirt. Though not as thick as on my exposed skin, a layer of grime has penetrated my garments. They lie stiff on the floor as though an invisible body is still inside. With some intense scrubbing, most of the filth washes off except for some stubborn spots on my elbows and knees and the crust under all my nails. The maid gathers up the soiled clothes and excuses herself.

When she exits, I lie back in the tub and shut my eyes. Warm water laps soothingly against my body. Thoughts immediately leap to the forefront of my mind as if they were waiting for my guard to go down so they could torment me. Even if we can overcome the mercenaries, my dilemma will remain—Liam is the sole heir to the throne, and we the king forbids us to marry. The kingdom needs him. Chaos will erupt if there is no clear successor to King William. A situation which will affect everyone both he and I love. He cannot abdicate this duty just for me.

For a split second, I contemplate joining Athos, until the heavy hollowness of his death crashes down on me. There will be no Athos to join. This is not the time to wallow in such thoughts, but my body has lost the will to move. In the shoulder deep water, I am overwhelmed, my eyes unfocused through the blur of tears, wishing the world would just swallow me up and be done with it.

A rap on the door breaks my stupor. Sally bustles in, her arms full. "Her Highness found these for you to wear."

She holds up a pair of small brown breeches and a white tunic. Grateful no one tried to put a corset back on me, I thank her, willing myself to stand. Once dried off and in the clean clothes, I feel refreshed. It takes several minutes for Sally to comb out the tangled rat's nest on my head. While I watch her coax still wet tresses into a braid, I notice how drawn and tired my reflection is.

Sally bustles out with the wet towels while I pull on some stockings. My dirty boots, which remain in the corner, are my only option for footwear. When I walk over to pick them up, I step on something hard. There on the floor is the rock Athos had given me after the king's rescue last fall. It must have fallen out of the pocket of my dirty breeches. I pick it up, rubbing the smooth surface with my fingers, a now cherished memento. With a heavy sigh, I put it in the pocket of my new pants.

Queen Helen awaits me in her main chamber. Together, we return to the throne room. My father is there, also freshly washed though without time to shave his beard. There are hollows in his face and his eyes sink deep beneath dark circles, but it all seems to vanish when he smiles at me. I run to his arms.

"Olivia," my mother's voice exclaims.

She is there with my sisters. They crowd around me, showering me with hugs and kisses. Lydia holds tightly around my legs. I pry my way out of her grip and kneel to hug her.

"I told you you could do it," she whispers with a note of triumph.

"Yes, you did." I squeeze her tighter.

"We cannot stay here," Mother explains. "They have prepared rooms elsewhere in the castle for family members. We just wanted a chance to see you and your father."

"What about Grace and Lucy?" I ask, worried they may have to fend for themselves.

"Don't worry. They are here as well in the servant's village," she replies to my relief. Everyone I care about is safe within the city walls.

A page steps forward and leads my family out of the room. My father remains next to me, his arm around my shoulder. The king stands at the head of a table with several advisors, who point at a large map of the city and surrounding area. Queen Helen is on the other side of the room, where she speaks with a handful of servants. Liam strides into the room and approaches us. He, too, is freshly cleaned and shaven.

"Sir Davenport," he exclaims, "how can I ever make up for the grievous actions of my cousin?"

In a rare breach of protocol, Father throws his arms around the prince. "My boy, I am so happy to see you alive. Your cousin's actions were his and his alone. There is nothing to make up for."

"And I am glad you are here to stand with us on the right side of this conflict," Liam answers. "I know who we both have to thank for that."

They smile at me, pulling me into their embrace. I want to share their joy, but the hollowness of earlier rears its head. Liam looks at me questioningly, just as King William calls everyone over. We part and join the group at the table, which now includes several knights, including Sir Michael, and a haggard looking scout. The queen comes to stand beside me.

"Sir Jack, please explain where we stand to everyone."

"We will station men on the parapets around the wall at strategic locations." He points to the map to indicate certain places. "Our strongest archers will be concentrated over the gate. behind them catapults loaded with boulders along with barrels of hot oil. More forces will be spread out along the top of the wall, but our forces are thin. We will not have the manpower to fill it, a fact which our enemy won't miss. If their numbers are too great, we won't be able to hold them for long."

King William studies the map thoughtfully for several moments, his fingers steepled by his lips. "I propose a small group ride out with me to meet with them. It may be our only chance to negotiate."

"A dangerous choice, but worth the risk, I believe," my father replies. "I will accompany you, of course."

"Yes," the king agrees, "and Sir Michael as well."

"And I," Liam adds, to a nod from all. "And Olivia."

"No," the monarch cries. "I will not put the girl in such peril."

"The girl you refer to is the reason we are all standing here now. She has more than earned her place at your side."

He puts his arm around my shoulder and stares his father down. I try to keep my face expressionless, but Liam's show of support warms my heart.

After a long deliberation, the king relents. "Very well."

"I worry they will not feel the need to negotiate at all once they see our scantily guarded walls and know they can overrun the city." Father states grimly.

King William sighs, his head down, though his eyes do not focus on the map in front of him. Silence hangs like a heavy cloud in the room.

"Unless…" I blurt, when I idea strikes me. Quickly, I bite my tongue. The king barely wants me to ride out with him. Surely, he does not want my unsolicited opinions.

"Unless what, Livy," my father coaxes.

"Well, what if they thought we had more soldiers than we actually have?"

Father's eyes brighten. "Like the Battle of Winchester?"

"Exactly."

There is a murmur of understanding from the group while father muses the idea, his brow knit in concentration. The others watch him expectantly. Finally, he turns to Sir

Michael. "What do you think? Do we have enough gear to make it believable?"

"It will be tough, but yes, from a distance, I think we do."

All eyes turn to the king for the final approval.

"It's the best shot we have. Send pages throughout the palace and village. Have the citizens gather in the main courtyard. I will address them in an hour's time. Meanwhile, Sir Michael, get to the armory and prepare the necessary equipment."

People break off in all directions, like ants scurrying from a broken nest.

"Liam," the monarch orders, "you come with me to discuss my address to the citizens. Sir Jack, take Olivia to the courtyard and await my arrival."

Liam takes my hand and kisses it and Queen Helen gives me a quick hug. As he passes me on his way out, the king puts his hand on my shoulder. "It's a good plan, Olivia. I only hope we can make it work."

26

Father and I make our way outside onto the main palace staircase. About halfway down, one step is wide enough to form a large landing before its followers descend to the bottom. Here, King William will address the people. Servants have cordoned off the area where he will stand with a heavy rope. Citizens already gather in the courtyard below and some even file onto the lower steps.

When we reach the landing, my father says, "Wait here. I am going to give orders to my men on crowd placement and control."

He strides off and soon speaks to a group of nearby soldiers, who stand smartly at attention in his company. The stay in prison must have left him tired and weak, but you would never guess. His presence is as commanding as ever.

I saunter to the side of the staircase and lean against a pillar. My stomach grumbles loudly, though a hearty meal does not seem to be in my immediate future. A blazing sun attempts to pierce high, hazy clouds with little luck. Humidity hangs thick in the air and soon my wet shirt clings to my back. This young summer looks to be as long and hot as we have seen in a long time, after all it is only June fifteenth. The date hits me like a flash—today would have been the wedding day of Harold and Emily. What a different path our lives have taken.

"Olivia!" a voice cries while arms fly around me.

"Kat. How are you?" I say, embracing her back heartily.

"Much better now that you and Puck are back safe and sound. And Liam too. Oh, Olivia, you must be so happy."

"Yes, I am," I say, even as the hollowness wells in my chest. My friend sees the flash of it in my eyes.

"What is it?"

"My friend, Athos, didn't make it." Not the whole truth, but enough to start.

She pulls me over to the side where we sit down on the stone ledge bordering the staircase, her arm around my shoulder. "Puck told me. I am so sorry. I know he meant a lot to you."

"Yes, he did." I whisper, fingering the stone in my pocket.

"Here are my two favorite ladies." Puck bounds over and the sadness flutters away. "There is no one else I would rather wait for an impending mercenary attack with."

Despite the serious circumstances, we all share a laugh. One of the many reasons I love my friend so much. He, too, found a chance to wash up and change back into his stable uniform. Quite unceremoniously, he pushes us apart and inserts himself in between us on the ledge. Kat and I elbow a side simultaneously while he wedges into the space.

"Was the Master-of-Horse mad at you for disappearing?" I query, knowing the man has little patience for rule breaking.

"Not at all. He is so grateful Prince Liam is alive and your father is innocent that he has been singing tavern songs like an old sot all afternoon."

As the crowd files into the courtyard, their combined voices grow from an indistinct murmur to a loud drone.

Servants, valets and stable hands arrive with their families in tow. Wives and mothers parade in, many with small children clinging to their legs or perched on their hip. Gray-haired men with canes and hunched over old ladies take up their positions. Courtiers and ladies come out of the palace and line the sides of the upper staircase right down to the landing. They pool around my two friends and me. The entire kingdom is represented in this audience.

Rumors spread like wildfire among the citizens; some who never had direct confirmation of Prince Liam's purported murdered. Only the highest echelon of nobles was informed, though gossip of this magnitude tends to bleed beyond its intended boundary. The mood is palpably uneasy while all heads crane to the door where their monarch will emerge.

When he finally materializes, flanked by Prince Liam and my father, an audible gasp rises, followed by a sudden silence. Queen Helen walks a few paces behind. Our eyes meet and she signals me to her side. Gently, I move through the nearby crowd, who saw the summons and step out of my path.

"Citizens of Stewartsland," King William begins just as I reach the queen's side, "Our kingdom has faced great peril from within. Prince Stephan, my own nephew, tried to usurp the throne."

Another audible gasp.

"I have dealt with him and his conspirators accordingly. However, we now face great peril from outside the kingdom. In his bid to overthrow me, Prince Stephan assembled an army on our northern shores. This force of mercenaries now marches toward our city and heavily outnumbers our own."

Panicked murmurs issue from some in the crowd. A few shout out in anger over the news. One woman wails dramatically from the courtiers. I look half expecting it to be my mother, who is well versed in theatrical hysterics, but it is a lady I do not recognize. Mother, I am happy to see, stands stoically along the wall next to my sisters. We catch each other's eye and she nods reassuringly. I give her a quick smile.

"The prince, Sir Davenport, and his daughter have devised a plan with which we hope to combat them."

Liam touches his father's arm. "May I?"

The king nods in assent, stepping to one side so his son can command the crowd's full attention. Every eye rests expectantly on Liam. In this moment, he will need to galvanize the kingdom; in this moment, he will need to show them how their future king can lead.

"My fellow countrymen, my brothers and sisters, many of you have heard rumors over the last week, I am sure. Now is the time to set the record straight. Prince Stephan, my only cousin, plotted against my father, our king. He staged my murder and framed Sir Davenport for the crime."

This time, they lace the gasp with disgust.

"His treachery ran deep and is counter to every belief we hold dear. He looked to gain this kingdom with the help of a paid army, soldiers loyal to only one thing—greed. His original plot involved Lord Otto, to whom he had promised the land of Lindenwood. Together, they wanted to ransom this beloved kingdom to an unethical king on the Mainland. The two of them would profit from the arrangement while we, the ordinary citizens, would be yoked into service for a foreign crown, levying steep taxes with no representation and little regard for the welfare of all but the chosen few."

His words hold the audience suspended in rapt attention. Not a sound can be heard but the booming of his voice. I have never seen him as regal as he does at this moment.

"Lord Otto, it seems, was expendable. When he became a liability, Stephan silenced him in what, at the time, looked to be in the defense of our king. He then used the death of my dear brother to further his plot. Thankfully, we discovered his plot and his true nature revealed."

The crowd applauds with shouts of "Long live the king" filling the courtyard. Liam holds up his hands to quiet them. There is more information to impart.

"Unfortunately, this is not where this story ends. Our very way of life is in peril. The mercenary army, which marches to attack, outnumbers us and we lack sufficient time to gather needed soldiers and resources from around the kingdom. If the attackers prevail, Stephan shall be freed, and his plan realized. Stewartsland faces a most formidable challenge."

Silence returns, the gravity of the situation bearing down on the people. Overhead, a lone hawk circles, its mighty wings spread across the blue sky. It sends out a mournful wail which echoes down to the uneasy crowd. Liam looks over his shoulder at me, the trepidation at what he needs to ask swimming in his eyes. I give him a nod of support.

He sets his shoulders and continues, "It is now I must confess the only way to win this fight will be as a kingdom. So, in this time of great crisis, we turn to you" The sea of faces before us looks somewhat baffled at this development, but they remain intent on their prince.

"If you would indulge me for a moment, I would like to tell you a story about a capital city much like Adelina, called Winchester. The people of this kingdom faced an attack from a large enemy army. In their moment of crisis, all hands took up arms to defend the city. The king disguised them all as soldiers and put them on the walls to defend the city. When their foe arrived, they were daunted by the great number of combatants who awaited them. The legion of both soldiers and civilians put up a fight which is now legendary in battle lore and defended their city from falling."

While he speaks, I see it—determination. It slowly fills the eyes of all, from the oldest crone to the young children barely old enough to understand what transpires. I have seen the look before, in training and in battle, the moment when your will decides how hard it wants to fight for something. My heart swells for Liam, for the king, for us all.

"And so, fellow citizens of Stewartsland, this is our Battle of Winchester. I, for one, will not see mercenaries defile our city. I will not see a traitorous coward upon the throne in the place of my father. I will not see this beautiful country corrupted by the greed of a Mainland king. So, I ask every able-bodied man and woman to take up arms and man the city walls. Let the hired army see the parapets filled with people who willingly defend their homeland and their beloved way of life. Who is with me?"

A tremendous cheer erupts from the crowd. King William steps to his son's side and pats him on the shoulder. Once again, the king raises his hands and silence falls quickly. He motions my father forward to address the populace.

"Citizens, we ask the elderly, sick, and mothers with their young children to gather in the main palace atrium. Queen Helen will see you safely sheltered from the fighting.

All others who wish to help report to the armory for further instructions."

"Go now," King William orders. "And may favor look kindly on Stewartsland and all who defend her."

After the ceremonial bows, the people disperse and although there is obvious concern for what the future holds, I am impressed by the orderliness and civility with which they carry themselves.

The three men head back to the palace. When they are a few steps past us, King William turns to me and says, "Come, Olivia. We must prepare to ride out."

Startled by the acknowledgement, I take a second to catch up with them. Liam slows his pace until I reach his side and we fall in step behind our fathers. Guards and courtiers part like the sea in front of us. Bartholomew rushes past in the other direction to the queen's side. She already distributes her orders for those who need a safe place to ride out the battle.

"How did I do?" Liam asks me.

"You were amazing."

"Yes, son," the monarch agrees. "You will make an admirable king one day."

"Thanks to Olivia," Liam insists.

Both men turn to beam at us with pride. Liam and I share a sideways smile with each other. For a moment, the fear of the approaching army fades. It is short lived. Pages run from different directions with a myriad of questions and problems. The anxiety of what we face hurtles back in.

Squires bring the king, Liam and my father their armor and help them dress. I watch restlessly from across the room. A hesitant hand taps my arm.

"Miss, for you." A young squire holds out a breastplate, forearm greaves, and a helmet. "Sir Michael sent these for you."

For a moment, I stare blankly at his timid face, his eyes round with apprehension. When the meaning sinks in, I can only marvel at the kind gesture by a man with whom I have had a fairly rocky relationship.

"Thank you, young man" I take the items from his outstretched arms.

"Let me help you," he offers, "and the name is Chet."

"I would appreciate that, Chet."

His motions are choppy, betraying his nerves. After I pull the breastplate over my head, he gets to work on the side laces. The irony of the moment strikes me, and I laugh out loud. Chet freezes like a child caught misbehaving. "Am I doing it wrong, Miss?"

"Not at all," I reply kindly, hoping to put him at ease. "It's just I once had a similar experience lacing up Sir Michael. Let's just say it didn't end well."

"Yes, Miss, I can believe that," he murmurs, strapping the greaves to my forearms.

"Sir Michael can be somewhat grumpy sometimes," I muse.

The boy will not denounce his superior in words, but the complicit grin he gives me conveys enough. "There. All set."

"Thank you, Chet. And promise to be careful if there is a battle. The kingdom needs brave squires like yourself."

"Yes, Miss, thank you, Miss," he stammers, handing me the helmet which I shove on my head. He bounds out of the room on to his next task.

Overall, the armor fits me quite well. Sir Michael clearly put some thought into it, which makes it all the more touching.

I stride over to a corner where Liam waits. He hands me my sword. Already in its belt, I strap it around my waist. He pulls off my helmet, my braid spilling down the front of one shoulder.

"Just like when we met," he teases, referring to my unmasking by Sir Michael on the Lindenwood mission.

"Technically, we met in the garden," I remind him.

"Yes, *technically*, of course. How could I forget?"

He leans in for a long kiss and the world melts away for a brief moment.

"Ready?" he asks.

"As I'll ever be."

He holds out a hand and we leave the room to join the king outside.

Horses await us at the bottom of the palace steps. In addition to the king, my father, Sir Michael, Liam and I, there are two standard bearers and one trumpeter.

Before I mount, I walk over to Sir Michael, high atop his steed. "Thank you for sending the armor. I truly appreciate it."

His gruff face stares down at mine, fixing me with the steely eyes which have sent shivers down even the most seasoned squire's spine. "It was well earned," he concedes, the slightest hint of a smile tugging at the corner of his mouth.

When I pull myself up into my saddle, Liam notices my wide grin and looks at me quizzically.

"It seems Sir Michael and I have officially buried the hatchet."

"Ah, well that's good news."

We share a laugh and kick the horses to a start. They trot past the palace to the front gate of the city. Nothing prepares me for the sight we face once we arrive.

Citizens of all ages and sizes prepare to defend their kingdom. Some have actual armor and weaponry. The rest have created their own—barrel tops for shields, kitchen knives and broomsticks for arms, and iron pots for helmets. Not only men, but women gather as far as the eye can see. Young and old line the ranks on the parapet overlooking the main gate and all around the surrounding walls. The senior knights direct people to strategic areas. People scurry up staircases and rush to bring supplies from the armory.

Torchlight illuminates the front gate held fast with iron bars. We come to a stop in front of it. King William surveys the scene. His chest puffed out with pride. "So many have come."

"Yes, Your Majesty," Father agrees, a satisfied gleam in his eyes.

"Let's go have a look from the parapet," the monarch says, swinging down off his steed.

We ascend the stone stairs hewn into the side of the stone wall. They zigzag the distance from one landing to another. At the top, people step aside so we can reach the edge. Gazing out across the flat expanse which leads up to the city gate, I discern a fine line of orange—the torches of the mercenary army. Slowly, it grows from a faint glowing blur to the outlines of men on horses and marching soldiers. About one hundred yards away, they halt, the snorting of the horses and the clank of armor clearly audible.

A group of three hulking men emerge on horseback. They gallop within ten yards of the gate and stop. Uneasy silence engulfs everyone on the parapet. The one in the center raises his head and booms, "Citizens of Adelina, we are here at the behest of Prince Stephan. Open the gate."

"We have a message to bring to you," my father shouts back, his voice reverberating off the stone.

The five of us quickly descend and mount our steeds. A team of men lifts the iron bar out of place, then turns the gears to open the gate. The heralds and trumpeter trot forward.

"Be sure to lock it once we are out," King William orders as we pass.

"Yes, Your Majesty."

Our horses hurry out to catch up with their cohorts. The gate slams shut behind us, the sound of the iron bar dropping into place rings across the plain. If this goes badly, we are sitting ducks. My heart pounds in time with the animal's steps.

I gaze over my shoulder up at the top of the wall. Torchlight illuminates every few feet, golden circles against the dark. From here, the space looks packed with soldiers, many men deep along the length of the edifice. Hopefully, our enemy will think a mighty force guards the city, when in reality only about a quarter of them are actual soldiers.

My horse whinnies, drawing my attention toward where the three men await us. As we come into view, they spot King William. One shifts uneasily in his saddle, a confused expression on his face. They are three of the biggest men I have ever laid eyes on. All look as though they enjoy destroying things just for the fun of it.

"What is this message?" the center one demands in a surly voice.

"The message," the king bellows, "is that my kingdom is firmly under my control. Your friend, Prince Stephan, has been exposed for the traitor he is. Currently, he rots in my prison awaiting execution. You no longer have any business here. Leave us in peace."

The men exchange looks, words passing silently among them. Their leader examines the wall and the locked gate. Time pounds on in loud seconds.

"We have come a long way," the mercenary finally says, "looting and burning as we went. My men are here to fight, not flee."

My heart sinks. How much of the land have they ravaged? An image of my parents' house comes to mind. Will it still be there when this is over?

If King William is upset by this statement, he does not flinch. Instead, he heaves a sigh, and, as though trying to explain something to a small child, says, "My army is prepared to fight and while you battle us, my brother's army from the south will close in on your rear, effectively trapping you."

The man's eyes narrow in consideration. Those of us who flank the king stare across with contrived confidence, hoping our enemy will buy the bluff.

"Prince Stephan controls the army from Prescott," he snorts. "Once they arrive, our forces will be even greater. If he is in your prison, they will rally with us to attain his release."

"No. Once they learned he planned to murder my son," our monarch assures falsely, gesturing to Liam, "they rallied around me. I have soldiers here who rode up from Prescott willing to confirm this information. Prince Stephan was the wrong person to put your faith in. If you await some sort of payment, none will be forthcoming."

The three men lean in close, conferring quietly with one another. We wait with breaths held in anticipation.

Finally, the leader turns back to us. "We believe we can take this city before the Prescott army arrives. We will release Stephan and claim what he promised to us."

"So be it," King William replies and kicks his horse to turn back to the city.

We follow while our adversaries return to their men. The front gate groans open in front of us and we quickly gallop through. As the iron bar slams back into place, all eyes are on the king. He surveys his citizens spread out in all directions around him.

"Good people of Stewartsland, prepare for battle," he orders.

Liam, a seasoned archer, posts himself right in the center of the parapet over the front gate with the rest of the city's best archers. The king and my father are nearby, each conveying orders for troop positioning. Too restless to stay still, I pace the walkway of the walls to get a feel for our defense.

Young men and women form a human chain on the staircases handing up large stones, which are laid into big piles at intervals along the wall. Franklin and Sadie stack one such mound. They are eager to show me their work, excited to help. Even Sally, the queen's timid maid, stands on the stairs passing the stones forward, a look of stern determination on her face.

Further along the wall, I run into Anne, Gretchen, and Elaine, who have all changed into breeches and tunics, long hair tied down under scarves. They pour thick dark oil into a large pot over a low flame. An older woman appears with a bucket of her own to dump in. She orders the others how to stir it properly. It takes me a full second to realize it's my mother.

"Oh, Olivia," she says noticing me, "we are heating this pot of oil to dump over on any of those nasty mercenaries who come too close to the wall. They will think twice about crossing us again."

Her eyes positively gleam with exhilaration. Anne catches my eye and suppresses a smile. My mother has always had a flair for the dramatic, but usually not in such a surprisingly helpful way.

"Just be careful," I warn. "They will shoot arrows over the wall. Be sure to stay out of range."

"Yes, dear," Mother says, taking my shoulders. "You be careful too."

"I will. Promise me if it gets bad, all of you will seek shelter inside."

They nod in unison and I hug each of them before returning to Liam's side. He gives me a comforting smile. Whatever happens, I want to be with him.

A horn blares from atop the wall, the signal of battle. I peek through a sight hole cut in the stone. The enemy runs across the empty plain toward the gate, battle cries emanating with a roar. They hold their shields high over head in defense of the many arrows which attempt to cut them down. Very few stumble and the sea of soldiers advances.

When they reach the wall, the front ranks part and several groups holding ladders run forward. They prop them against to wall and some attempt to climb. Arrows still fly at the bulk of the army on the field. But now, our people throw the stones at the climbers, whom they pelt from all sides. Several lose their balance and fall to the ground, where others are fast to take their place.

More ladders emerge from the churning deep below. A few stalwart enemies reach the top, where they breach the wall. Our men meet them and sword fights break out. Despite the laborious efforts of the stone throwers, more men reach the tops of the ladder.

A thick man jumps over the wall just a few feet from me. It is imperative to keep our foes away from the archers who provide our best defense at the moment. I race over with my sword drawn and our weapons clang together with force. Several more men jump onto the platform and additional soldiers come forward to meet them.

Fighting at such close quarters is difficult. Swords and bodies fly all around me. While I parry with my rival, someone elbows me in the head, whether it is one of them or one of us, I do not know. The blow may have knocked me off balance, but I am so close to the wall, it braces the impact.

An agonizing scream pierces the night when the vats of hot oil douse the men. For a split second, everyone freezes before continuing on with even more fervor. There are people all around me now. In the dark, it is hard to make out more than outlines. My foe gets pushed forward and loses his footing. I use the opportunity to drive the hilt of my sword into the side of his oncoming head. He collapses to the ground.

Swinging my sword back to the ready position, I look for my next fight. In front of me, the archers maintain their assault from the ledge. Beneath them, men fight hand to hand while our citizens still hurl stones and dump hot oil over the side of the wall. It is a sight like I have never seen before in my life. There is not time to worry about my family or Liam or anyone, for that matter. All I can do is try to hold off the next man who leaps in front of me. For the moment, my adrenaline over fuels my exhaustion, but in the back of my mind, I know the longer this goes on, the worse it will be for my kingdom.

Trumpets sound from far off, likely some sort of mercenary signal. It is too soon for anyone from Prescott to arrive. A new opponent steps forward to meet me, the clash of our swords vibrating me to my very core. Before long, he has me backed against the wall, a vicious barrage of blows coming down on me. His weapon flies close and I feel a gash open on my cheek.

Suddenly, there is a loud *thunk* and he pulls back. Another follows. Anne and Gretchen throw stones at the man's head in an effort to aid me. The distraction works long enough for me to elbow the man under his chin and knock him off balance. I scramble away from the wall to where my sister and her accomplice stand. My foe regains his steadiness and turns on the three of us. Using my body as a shield, I step between him and the others, prepared to protect them at all costs. In the torchlight, he looms, a giant silhouette poised to strike.

Trumpets blare again, this time from several directions. Men stationed on the watch towers yell, "Surrender. They hold the flag of surrender." All fighting ceases, the enemy soldiers exchanging bewildered looks. The mercenary army has relinquished the fight. But why?

"Olivia, what's going on?" my sister whispers.

"I don't know. Stay here while I find out."

I head back to the area of the wall over the main gate. Father is there with Sir Michael and the king. Heads bowed together, they confer about the situation. Just as I arrive, Liam approaches from the other direction. We embrace and he looks with concern at the gash on my face.

"It seems their leadership would like to speak with us again," my father informs us.

"Some sort of trap?" the prince asks.

"Unlikely. Apparently, someone arrived in our defense at the back of their lines and they yielded the fight."

"Who?" I ask the question on everyone's mind.

"Let us find out," our monarch says.

Once again, we saddle our horses. Absently, I wipe my bloodied cheek on my sleeve just before mounting. We trot out through the open gate. Our enemy has pulled back, leaving a wide swath between them and the wall. The trio of men from earlier awaits us a little in front of their troops. First, three other riders approach us from the side, one holding a standard of King William. They come to a stop in front of us.

"Your Majesty," says Luke with a bow. Bryan and Pat flank him, the latter bearing the standard. "We took it upon ourselves to gather some men. There are many out there loyal to our band. We met the enemy from the rear. Once the mercenaries learned of Athos' death and Prince Stephan's part in it, their allegiance quickly changed."

Unsurprisingly, Athos commanded a significant amount of respect and loyalty from other outlaws and mercenaries. His reputation for fairness and assistance was known far and wide. When our enemy faced an attack on two fronts and realized Athos' own men were against them, the ranks quickly had a change of heart about continuing to defend Prince Stephan.

"Thank you, although this alone does not seem adequate," King William says. "Now let us get these invaders out of Stewartsland.

The enemy leaders silently appraise us upon our arrival. Ever the mercenary, the largest one says, "We will retreat to Lindenwood and leave the island. However, as I have many mouths to feed, more looting will likely occur. What am I to do?" He spreads his hands ingenuously.

"A legion will escort you to our borders. We will provide the necessary fare for the journey. No more of our land will be touched."

"Agreed," the man replies, knowing how well they make out with this deal. It is a large concession by the king, but ultimately, he just wants to be rid of them. "One more thing, we have something of Prince Stephan's we would rather be rid of. We leave it to you to take care of the matter."

He signals to the men behind him and one lone horseman breaks forward, someone on the saddle behind him. When he stops, he pushes his passenger to the ground. Scrambling to her feet is Emily Crawford, her eyes wide with confusion.

"Ah, Emily," Liam drawls, "Prince Stephan awaits you in the citadel."

Her eyes fill with tears but for once her mouth stays shut. One of our heralds dismounts and installs her atop his horse, which he walks back toward the gate. King William and the enemy leader stare at each other one long, last moment. Our foe kicks his horse to a turn and goes back to join his waiting men.

The monarch steers around to our city gate. "Jack, put a group together for the escort. Sir Michael, you will lead it up north."

"Yes, Your Majesty," they reply in unison.

We return through the front gate, where squires wait to take our horses. Soldiers of Stewartsland have rounded up the opponents and herded them into one area of the courtyard. My father instructs the guards to release them. They hurry away without a look back. Liam hugs his father, relief written all over his face. Father shakes hands with Sir Michael, then pulls me into an embrace. The herald stands by with Emily, who looks travel-stained and weary.

"Please, Your Majesty," she gasps, "have mercy on me."

The king throws up a hand to silence her. "Get her out of my sight."

A soldier drags her away, the crowd parting quickly for them. Her sobs echo off the stone walls until they fade into nothingness. My father and Sir Michael depart to carry out their orders. Liam and I follow in the king's wake toward the palace steps. Queen Helen rushes down into her husband's open arms.

At a tap on my arm, I find Sadie, Franklin at her side. She and I share an embrace, her happy tears falling against my neck. Liam shakes the boy's hand profusely, thanking him for all his help. Franklin nods furiously, his eyes full of wonder at the acknowledgement.

"Livy," a voice shrieks and Lydia wraps around my lower half. Ellen, Grace, and Lucy soon join her. All three of them helped fortify the back walls during the fight. They breathlessly tell me their adventures, interrupting each other often.

"They made me sit in a stupid room with a bunch of other kids doing nothing," Lydia complains.

"Someday, you will have your chance," I assure her.

My mother and Anne find us, both completely disheveled, but eyes bright with the thrill of their escapades on the wall. They add their stories to the mix. Then, mother becomes somber. "I am worried for Jayne," she sniffs. My eldest sister and her husband, Lord Davis, were summering at their country estate on the river. Hopefully, their property was spared from the looting.

Montgomery arrives, his tunic torn to shreds on one side, the detached sleeve dangling down by his waist. He and Anne hug and they too worry about his family and their home in the country.

Yet these cares do not dampen the merriment. The victory coupled with the reunion of loved ones buoys the mood of everyone. All around us, celebrations break out. Citizens shed their armor, both real and makeshift. Bonfires are lit and men carry out kegs of ale and open them in the street.

We sit in a cluster on a section of the palace steps. Even mother partakes in a glass of celebratory ale. Kat and Puck find us, both filthy, yet smiling nonetheless. They share their battle stories as readily as the others had. Servants bring food from the palace and pass it around, no one is in a hurry for the night to end.

Liam has disappeared with his parents for the moment. A sense of peace fills me; he is where he should be. If I have to let him go to fill his destiny, I can. It will hurt. I will grieve for a long time and my heart will never truly recover. I may never feel the total completeness I feel with him, but sitting here with my family and friends makes me realize that even without him, I am still enough.

The next few weeks are a flurry of activity. Sir Michael and a battalion escort the mercenary army back to the coast. Without the promised pay from Prince Stephan, their time is now wasted. They cause no problems and the trip concludes without incident. Where they head next is surely someone's problem, but not ours. We have our own issues to deal with.

Large portions of the countryside were ravaged and burned. Many peasants lost all their meager possessions. Liam spearheads a group of young men who erect modest, yet adequate shelters for these families. Troops arrive from the south and get to work on clearing all charred and broken items left on roadways and in fields. Nobles, whose estates were looted, see to their properties, indexing what they lost. My family's home lost our barn and several fields burned black. Workers help restore broken buildings all around the kingdom in an effort organized by Puck, who steps grandly up to the challenge.

Niobe and I see to many citizens, both within the city walls and from the countryside, dispensing herbs, salves or just an ear willing to listen and empathize. We enlist both Kat and my sister, Ellen, for assistance. The latter shows a remarkable aptitude for the healing arts.

The sense of community and the spirit of cooperation all around uplift me, even during two arduous hurdles I must cross.

First is the burial of Athos. King William allows his men to choose a location for his grave. They select a plot of land at the top of a rise, under the boughs of a stately oak tree. On a clear day, from its summit, the shimmering ribbon of the Crystal River shines below, flowing endlessly out to the sea.

Luke asks Liam and me to attend the small service. King William joins us as discreetly as his station allows. Athos' men take turns eulogizing him. Although there is much I had wanted to say, my tears sweep away the words. The prince expresses how much he meant to both of us. When all seems finished, the king steps forward.

"I cannot say as many of you can that I counted Athos as a friend. Our positions in life were, by nature, adversarial. This does not mean he has not earned my utmost admiration. I knew of him from his days on the Mainland, where he was a decorated general, until he was accused of crimes against his king and exiled. Years later, evidence arose to clear his name, but he chose not to return to his homeland. Though I may not condone all aspects of the *trade* he practiced here in Stewartsland, I am struck by his heart. He came to my aid and then the aid of my son. He did not let the betrayals of his past harden him to the point of not caring about his fellow humans. These were principals he upheld until his death. It serves as a powerful lesson to all, especially to me. May he rest in peace."

A few days later, Luke gathers his men to lead them north. King William asked for the men act as a special legion for the northern borders by Lindenwood. Though not officially part of the army, they would receive a stipend every year for their troubles. On our parting, Luke takes my hand and kisses it. When he releases his grip, something remains in my hand. While he mounts and they trot away, I look down at the new stone in my hand, a symbol meaning I can now come to him in any time of need. My eyes fill with tears as I clasp it to my heart.

The second difficult day is the one of the executions. In all, forty men and one woman are put to death. All the lesser men are hung in a large group, but Prince Stephan and Emily are beheaded in the city square. On this day, anyone in the kingdom has the opportunity to witness the spectacle. I choose not to. Even though in my heart there is anger at both of them, I do not wish to have their final horrible minutes on earth branded in my brain forever.

Instead, I ride out Pepper with Lydia holding on tight behind me for a picnic. We stop at a pond with an idyllic waterfall emptying into its far side. Lydia immediately decides it is fairy territory. We spend our afternoon searching for the elusive creatures, much to my sister's delight. In the evening, when Liam and I are finally together, he looks drawn and weary.

"It is better you did not see it, Olivia," is all he says of the day's events.

Gradually, a sense of normalcy returns. I move back into my room in the palace, though I am hardly there but to sleep. The king never says a word about Liam and me. Eventually the news will come, a dark cloud on the periphery of my mind. But with each passing day, life settles into a routine.

One morning, Anne and I sit in our room while Sadie brushes out my sister's hair. They discuss the servant's recent engagement to Franklin, exchanging wedding ideas. I reach over and grab my second sweet roll.

"Be careful," Anne teases. "You are so pleased to be back in shape. Those won't help."

I stick out my tongue and Sadie erupts into a fit of giggles. It is almost as though nothing ever happened, as though we would go find Kat and lounge in the gardens to complain about the heat. But the loss is there, a deep hole still to be reckoned with. I sigh at the thought of Harold, Adam, Athos, and an innocence this court will never know again.

Anne's eyes narrow, but before she can question me, there is a rap on the door. Sadie hops over to answer it. A page steps in. "Pardon me ladies, but King William wishes to speak to Miss Olivia. I am here to escort her."

Though I knew the moment was coming, it takes me by surprise. Still in my nightgown, we send him back to the hall to wait. Our maid flies to my wardrobe, hair pins for my sister still clenched in her teeth. Since returning to the castle, I have spent most days with Niobe roving the countryside and have taken to wearing the breeches and tunics worn by the servant boys. They are easy to walk and bend in and far less costly to replace when soiled.

"I'm afraid you won't find anything suitable in there, Sadie."

"You are welcome to anything of mine," Anne offers, "though the fit will be off."

My sister is both taller and bustier than I.

"Maybe I could pin it," Sadie proposes, almost frantic at the prospect of making me look presentable.

A few months ago, I would have shared her panic, worried about making the perfect impression on His Majesty. Now, however, those feelings don't exist. I am who I am.

"I'll just wear my day dress and you can put my hair in a bun."

Sadie removes the shapeless, black dress from its hanger, and I slip it on. She coils my hair into a tight bun at the nape of my neck. The maid takes extra care with the simple hairstyle as though it may somehow make all the difference in my overall appearance. When finished, she and my sister look at me with apprehension.

"Are you sure this is how you want to go?" Anne voices the thought etched on both their faces.

"Yes. If he doesn't accept who I am by now, then so be it."

"Are you nervous?" she asks, her hand coming to rest on mine.

"Yes. But better to just get it over with once and for all."

The page jumps to attention when I walk into the hall. He, too, gives my attire a dubious glance, but says nothing. We set off at a brisk pace, down one corridor, up some stairs and around several corners until we stop outside the king's chambers. Liam sits on a bench against the wall near the closed doors. He dismisses the page, who scurries off like a frightened rabbit and Liam rises.

When he takes me into his arms, my heart sinks. All those weeks back, I vowed to let Liam go if his father forces him to marry another. The kingdom will not survive without a prince to inherit the throne. Now that the moment is here, my resolve wavers.

"Come," he says, taking my hand to lead me forward.

A guard opens the door and I take a deep, quivering breath. We step over the threshold. King William sits at a large, mahogany desk, its front intricately carved with his emblem, two boars flanking a mighty oak. Sunlight pours in through a bank of windows whose transoms are stained glass, dappling the floor with splatters of color. Queen

Helen stands by them looking out onto the courtyard, a dark silhouette against the bright rays.

"Come in, you two, have a seat," the monarch instructs.

We ease into the two chairs facing the desk, never releasing hands. The queen strolls over to stand behind her husband, her face unreadable.

"I apologize for taking so long to speak with you both," the king says.

"Given the circumstances, it's entirely understandable" his son replies, a clipped cadence belying the courteous words. It is the first chink in confidence Liam has shown about our future together.

"Well, I could not be more pleased with our progress. Everyone has contributed to the restoration of the kingdom, down to the last man."

"Indeed, it has been wonderful to see," Liam agrees, "but that is not what we are here to talk about."

"No, I suppose not," he concedes and takes a deep breath. "I will be honest; my opinion has not changed. I believe as the sole heir, your marriage should be used as an opportunity for alliance."

The room seems to shrink in size around me, squeezing all the air from my lungs. Liam makes to protest but his father holds up a hand.

"I am not finished. Olivia, I want you to know this is in no way a reflection of my opinion of you. You, my dear, are an incredible young woman. In fact, your spunk reminds me much of my Helen in her youth." He bestows a loving look on his wife.

"Thank you, Your Majesty," I whisper, then clamp my trembling lips shut.

Liam leaps to his feet. "I've already told you I won't live without her. If you send her away, you will lose me, too."

This is where I should speak, should tell him to choose the correct path—the one which does not include me—for the sake of all the citizens of Stewartsland. My voice, however, is silent.

"Yes, my son, I don't think anyone is in any way unclear about your feelings. But again, I was not finished."

The prince sinks back down next to me and I retake his hand in mine.

"Although that is my practical opinion, I realize any arranged marriage would result in an empty alliance which would not benefit Stewartsland in the long run. An unhappy king makes the poorest of monarchs. Therefore, I think it would be best for all concerned if the two of you marry."

The tiniest smile forms at the corners of the queen's mouth while we try to digest what the king has just said. They both wait for the shock to dissipate. It takes a few seconds to sink in, but when it does, Liam howls in delight. He picks me up in an embrace and swings me around. Queen Helen is next. While hugging and thanking her, the door opens, and my parents are escorted in. Mother, already in tears, clearly knows the news. Father beams with pride and shakes the king's hand.

To my surprise, the king embraces me. "Welcome to the family, young lady."

"Thank you, Your Majesty," I whisper again, trying to hold back tears, though tears of joy this time. It does not work, and they flow freely down my cheek.

Father whips out a handkerchief. After years of practice with my mother, he is never without one. Liam puts an arm around my waist and pulls me to the comfort of his side.

"Thank you, Father," he says.

"Well, in the end," the monarch replies with a wink, "I figured it was best to keep Olivia around in case one of us needs rescuing again."

Everyone bursts out laughing, even the stoic guards who stand by the doorway. A valet enters with champagne and glasses and there are toasts all around.

Liam pulls me aside. "A toast to you, my future wife. You rescued my heart the moment I first saw you in the garden."

"You mean when I was lying on the ground covered in dirt?" I tease.

"Exactly," he laughs, and we share a long kiss.

Between the champagne and the pure bliss, my feet don't touch the ground.

I top off a vial with the last of the peppermint oil. Niobe quietly prepares a tincture at my side. "We will need more of this." I wave the empty bottle in the air. "Well, you will." Sadness is evident in my tone.

The healer wraps an arm around me. "There, there, child, it's not as though you are leaving the kingdom entirely. You are welcome here anytime."

With the announcement of my engagement, many changes were required of me. One was to cease being Niobe's assistant. Apparently, there are more important duties for a princess. My sister Ellen, who showed such aptitude for the healing arts, will take my place. While thrilled at the assignment, the prospect of moving into the castle daunts her, much like it did me all those months ago. She sits on my other side, as she has for the past week, watching my every move.

"Yes, I will have to make sure my sister is a worthy replacement," I joke, attempting to lighten my mood.

Today is my last day working with my beloved friend. I place the vial in the basket used for the village rounds. Rising in unison, we remove our aprons. Wistfully, I hang mine on its peg. We open the door and step out into the late summer heat. The sky is a perfect blue canvas, not even a cloud to smear its grandeur.

"Are you sure you remember what to do?" I question Ellen.

"Yes, Livy. I had an excellent teacher."

"Maybe I should come again."

"No, dear," the witch replies. "You said all your goodbyes yesterday. Remember? Though again, it is not as if you are leaving us, for goodness sake. You will now be in a position to look after the villagers in an even greater capacity."

"I know," I concede. "I'll just miss it."

She pulls me into an embrace, her frame finally feeling a little more solid to me. "You were a special gift to me, Olivia. I will always look back on our time fondly. And while I will miss your daily company, I will be even more proud to see you as my princess."

"Thank you. You were a life saver to me in more than one way," I manage, my voice shaky with emotion.

"Now go. You have many more important tasks to deal with today."

My wedding is tomorrow. For a whirlwind six weeks, the kingdom has planned the event. The queen, right down to the most meager servant, tapped in some way for preparations. At this point, the well-oiled planning machine hardly seems to need me so long as I show up at the appointed hour in the morning. But I would like to spend one more afternoon with Liam.

"All right." I say. "I'll see you at home later, Ellen."

My sister nods. Niobe embraces me once more, then rubs my cheek affectionately before turning toward the village.

There is still some time before Liam will be free, so I head to the stables. Puck is outside the barn giving instructions to a few young underlings. His standing has risen dramatically since we returned, clearly now the successor to the Master-of-Horse. The boys run off in different directions when he finishes speaking.

"Hey there, Livy—I mean, Princess Olivia."

"First of all, I am not officially a princess until tomorrow. Second of all, don't call me that. It doesn't feel right."

"I don't think I get a choice in the matter," he laughs. "I'm sure it will grow on you."

"We shall see."

He takes my hand and leads me into the shady stable, where we plop on two hay bales. All the stalls burst at the seams with horses ridden here by wedding guests. Most stand quietly in the heat, their tales fanning away the flies. A few munch eagerly on some hay. The ordinariness of it all comforts me. It reminds me of all the simple times shared with Puck over the years. True to form, he leans back, content with the comfortable silence between us. Nothing needs to be said. Nothing ever has. We just get each other.

"If I get stuck with one more pin, I will hurt someone," Kat exclaims, suddenly standing before us.

"Bad dress fitting?" I ask. Kat will be one of my bridesmaids tomorrow.

"Long. But done finally."

She sits down next to Puck and they lean against one another. Absently, she picks a strand of hay from his hair. It warms my heart seeing them together.

"Done for this one. We still have Anne's and yours to go," I remind her.

In the fall, she and my sister will be married only two weeks apart. Our kingdom will not be wanting for wedding celebrations any time soon. Puck popped the question last week, much to everyone's delight. The cascade of good news was so welcome after all which had transpired.

"I'm sure glad I'm not a girl," Puck muses. "All I have to do is put on my best suit and show up."

With a conspiratorial look between us, Kat and I each grab a handful of hay and toss it at him.

"What?" he laughs. "It's not my fault I get off easy in the deal."

We all laugh, the two of us helping dust the hay off of him. For an hour, we joke and talk as though it is any other day, just the respite I needed from the eternal planning. At length, I rise.

"I have to go meet Liam now."

They both stand and embrace me in turn.

"Thank you, Kat, for being such a dear friend. The palace would have been a much lonelier place without you," I whisper in her ear.

"I feel the same," she says. "I know you are my friend, but even if you weren't, I can't think of a better princess for this kingdom than you."

"Agreed," says my oldest friend, wrapping me in his arms. "But don't worry, you will always be Livy to me."

"I wouldn't have it any other way, Puck. See you two tomorrow."

"Wait until you see Salozo," Liam says. "The streets are canals the people navigate by boat. What a sight! It will be my favorite stop on the trip."

He has spent days detailing all the cities we will visit on the Mainland for our honeymoon. Nervous excitement fills me about traveling there. I have never been off of Stewartsland, whereas Liam has made the journey several times.

"Is the water deep?" I ask, trying to imagine such a place.

"Less than ten feet, I am told. Why are you worried? You know how to swim."

"Thankfully, one of us does," I tease.

We sit in the archery yard, the late summer sun taking its time across the sky. For a while we shoot at targets, but we both find it difficult to concentrate, the weight of tomorrow's ceremony lingering on our minds.

"It will be nice to have some time to ourselves," he comments.

Between the restoration of the outer villages and the constant nuptial decisions, time alone has been scarce. Even now, Liam's attendant stands nearby, my old friend Seth, newly promoted to the position. I look at him and sigh heavily.

"You are thinking of Adam?" Liam murmurs, always able to read my thoughts. "Me too. I wish he was here. He would have been my best man with my brother gone. Not only will we make sure Liza is well taken care of from now on, but Charlie's future will be looked after as if he were one of our own. I owe that to his memory."

Tears form in the corners of my eyes. The grief still comes and goes in waves, sometimes only a tiny drip and others an entire deluge of emotions. Our wedding has been a welcome distraction from more somber thoughts, not just for me, but for many in the kingdom.

"No more talk of sadness," he exclaims, pulling me to my feet. "There has been too much of it these past months. Let's practice our first dance."

Like everything else related to the ceremony, there were rules about exactly what dance we have to perform, a good luck tradition connected to it somehow. Though not complicated, my anxiety about performing it in front of an audience makes the dance seem harder. Only a few moves in and I step on Liam's foot. I tense with frustration.

"Don't worry," he assures. "A minor mistake like that will hardly be noticeable."

"Liar," I accuse, and he laughs.

"Excuse me, Your Highness." Sir Michael strolls across the grass toward us, a leather folder in his hand.

"Ah, Sir Michael, how are all your preparations coming along?" Liam asks.

With Prince Stephan dead, King William decided to send the senior knight to Prescott to act as its steward. He has spent the last few weeks setting his affairs in order.

"All but done now," he replies, holding out the folder to Liam. "Here are my status reports on every knight, down to the last squire. I hope you find it helpful."

"I'm sure I will. Is Constance ready for the move?"

"Yes, as any dutiful wife, she has packed twenty times more than necessary. I've assured her shops exist in Prescott, but she is taking no chances."

We chuckle. In all the time I have known Sir Michael, it never occurred to me he had a wife. At his promotion, she had been by his side, an attractive older woman. Funny how you can know only one side of someone.

"We look forward to seeing you both tomorrow," I say.

"It will be our pleasure," the knight responds. "And, if I may get personal for a moment, I want you both to know how happy I am for you. Miss Olivia, I have known the prince since he was a boy and I could not imagine a better match for him than you."

Spontaneously, I embrace him and receive a powerful hug in return. He then excuses himself, leaving me a bit dumbfounded by the entire exchange.

"Well, that was quite different from our first meeting right over there." I point around the hedges toward the little used garden.

"When he picked you up like a sack of potatoes?" Liam jokes.

"Don't remind me. Let's just be happy we've mended our fences."

The tower clock strikes five, its resonant chime echoing across the air. It is time for me to go. We linger a few more moments, exchanging stolen kisses until someone clears their throat behind us. Madame Le Clare comes to fetch me. After one more quick embrace, Liam and I draw apart."

"I guess I'll see you tomorrow," I say.

"I will be the handsome devil waiting at the altar," he says with a wink.

The headmistress puts her arm around my shoulder and steers me away. Liam's eyes stay connected with mine until the last possible second, every unspoken thought and feeling sensed between us. How lucky I am to have found someone who loves me so well.

Madame Le Clare sets out at a brisk pace through the hallways and I stagger to keep up. Eventually, she comes to an outer door, pushing it open with her usual clipped motions. A carriage waits. It will take me to my parent's house to spend this last night.

"Maids will come to your home early tomorrow to help you dress. Three carriages will be sent to bear you and your family back here."

"Thank you." A footman holds the door open for me.

"Don't be nervous and try to get enough sleep," the headmistress instructs, her tone almost motherly, unusual for her to say the least.

"I will." I step into the vehicle and settle onto the seat. "Thank you for all your help."

"Remember, princesses must strive to be perfect. It's protocol, after all." She shuts the door, walking away in her usual brusque manner.

Something tells me I won't be the type of princess she is comfortable with.

Home is a madhouse of activity. Gowns, ribbons, shoes, and jewelry lay strewn on every surface. Anne oversees the bedlam, relaxed and in her element. Mother is in the midst of selecting a hairstyle for tomorrow. Her maid stands over her with an assortment of hairpins in hand.

"I liked it better when it was all up," Anne tells the maid, who gets back to work on my mother's locks. "Here, Ellen, try this one next."

My less than thrilled sister takes a blush colored gown out of her hands. Lydia sits on the floor, petticoats engulfing her like a luscious ring of whipped cream. Her feet stick out from the frills, one in a blue shoe, and the other in a pink one. She attempts to play jacks, but the small metal pieces stick to her garments.

"Hi, Livy," she welcomes, a tired edge to her voice.

I wave at her around the ever-flowing chain of humans who circle the room. Grace enters with an armful of gowns, trailed by Lucy, who holds a box full of scarves and ribbons. My eldest sister, Jayne, follows behind them. Thankfully, her home suffered little damage in the attack.

She gives me a quick hug before dashing off to follow one of Anne's orders.

"I thought all of this was decided already," I comment to the sister in charge.

"There's always room for improvement," Anne replies. "Besides, how often will I get to prepare for a royal wedding?"

"Let's hope not for a long while. Do you need me for anything?"

"No. Your outfit is the only one set to go."

Relieved to avoid the chaos, I head for my father's office. The door stands ajar, a thick cloud of cigar smoke billowing into the hall. Laughter follows and the voices of Jayne's husband and Anne's fiancé. Not wanting to intrude, I wander out into the garden off the kitchen. Though humid out, an awning shades it from the late afternoon sun. A mixture of herb scents vie with each other: mint, sage, and basil.

The last time I sat here, the world was in disarray—Father arrested, Liam missing and presumed dead, the kingdom without an heir—such a contrast to today. And though I will marry my prince tomorrow, I do not expect a "happily ever after". Life has shown this to be a childish and unrealistic notion. Liam and I will face good days such as these last few weeks, and bad ones as we have braved before. There is no good without the bad and hard times make one appreciate the enjoyable ones rather than expecting smooth sailing at all times.

So much of our future lies in uncharted waters. I will be the first non-royal to inherit the title of princess and one day queen. My work with Niobe will end while Ellen gradually takes my place. Liam and I plan to continue not only my training but offer it to other girls in the kingdom.

The performance of women on the night of the attack inspired the king to let us try it.

While there are many good times ahead, there will be bumps in the road, sometimes more than bumps. We have already been through times where the road seems to disappear entirely. Yet, there is no one I would rather take this journey with, no other shoulder I would rather cry on, no other arms I want to feel around me at day's end. If nothing else, of this I am sure.

So, when the night fades to a morning of whirlwind activity, the surety keeps me calm. From the dressing, to the carriage ride, to the chapel doors, it buoys me.

And when Father, in his best uniform, grazes my cheek with one last kiss just as two servants pull open the doors, says, "You were always a princess to me. I hope you will be truly happy, my Olivia."

I look down the aisle past the spectators to where Liam awaits, a broad smile on his face, and can honestly answer, "I know I will be."

About the Author

Jane McGarry cannot remember a time she did not love reading and this progressed into a passion for writing. She lives in New Jersey in a house full of boys and two over-indulged cats. In her rare quiet moments, she can be found curled up with said cats and a good book.

You can visit her online at janemcgarrybooks.com

Clean Reads
GREAT STORIES. NO GUILT.
www.cleanreads.com

www.ingramcontent.com/pod-product-compliance
Lightning Source LLC
Chambersburg PA
CBHW031444200726
48289CB00007BB/2209